Lacey Miles sto... her only reaction u signt narrowing of her eyes.

"Ms. Taylor said you had specified that you had no issues with hiring a male caretaker."

"I don't," she said bluntly in a tone that suggested just the opposite.

"You seem as if you've been blindsided."

Her lips curved in a faint, perfunctory smile. "I guess I have been, in a way. I didn't have a chance to look over your credentials or even get your name. I just wasn't expecting a man."

"Oh."

"I'm in a hurry to make a hire, you see," she added quickly, as if she realized what she'd just admitted made her sound ill prepared. "In fact, you're the first person who's even applied for the job."

He was pretty sure he knew why. The story about the car bomb meant for her, the one that had killed her sister and brother-in-law instead, had made the national news. There weren't a lot of wannabe nannies willing to walk into a situation like that. Which made him the perfect person for the job.

OPERATION NANNY

PAULA GRAVES

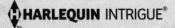

For my nieces, Sarah, Kathryn, Melissa and Ashlee, and my nephew, Nathan. Most of you aren't old enough to read my books, but maybe you'll look them up in a few years, see this dedication and smile.

ISBN-13: 978-0-373-75670-4

Operation Nanny

Copyright © 2017 by Paula Graves

PLEASE RECYCLE

Recycling programs for this product may not exist in your area.

HARLEQUIN®
™ www.Harlequin.com

Printed in U.S.A.

Paula Graves, an Alabama native, wrote her first book at the age of six. A voracious reader, Paula loves books that pair tantalizing mystery with compelling romance. When she's not reading or writing, she works as a creative director for a Birmingham advertising agency and spends time with her family and friends. Paula invites readers to visit her website, paulagraves.com.

Books by Paula Graves

Harlequin Intrigue

Campbell Cove Academy

Kentucky Confidential
The Girl Who Cried Murder
Fugitive Bride
Operation Nanny

The Gates: Most Wanted

Smoky Mountain Setup
Blue Ridge Ricochet
Stranger in Cold Creek

The Gates

Dead Man's Curve
Crybaby Falls
Boneyard Ridge
Deception Lake
Killshadow Road
Two Souls Hollow

Visit the Author Profile page at Harlequin.com for more titles.

CAST OF CHARACTERS

Lacey Miles—A network reporter and the target of an unknown assailant who set a car bomb that killed her sister and brother-in-law, leaving her to take care of her small niece.

Jim Mercer—Hired by Lacey to be a live-in nanny for her niece, the former marine has a hidden agenda.

Katie Harper—Lacey's two-year-old niece has just lost her parents. Will being with Lacey put her in danger?

Detective Bolling—The Arlington County police detective is investigating the bombing that killed Lacey's sister and brother-in-law.

Alexander Quinn—The Campbell Cove Academy CEO has a connection with Jim Mercer. What is his real interest in Lacey's case?

al Adar—The terrorist group once wrought havoc across the Central Asian nation of Kaziristan before it fell out of favor. Now trying to refashion itself into a global threat, has the group focused on Lacey as its first high-profile target?

Justin and Carson Whittier—Lacey did a series of investigative reports into allegations against the handsome, charismatic brothers running for Congress from Connecticut. Are they influential enough—and ruthless enough—to target Lacey for murder?

J. T. Swain—Lacey's investigation into the mysterious backwoods gangster has turned up the heat on this fugitive. Are the attempts on Lacey's life his retaliation?

Chapter One

The blue pickup truck was in her rearview mirror again. It had been there, off and on, since shortly after she'd crossed the Potomac into Maryland. Of course, many vehicles—not just the pickup—had shared the road into Frederick with her, many of them staying behind her for miles at a time before turning off.

Maybe that was the problem, Lacey thought. The pickup had never turned off.

A soft whine from the backseat drew her attention away from the rearview mirror. She dared the quickest glance at the child seat belted in behind the passenger seat, reassuring herself that Katie was just being fussy. Her niece's bright gray eyes stared back at Lacey, reminding her so much of Marianne that she had to suck in her breath against a sharp stab of grief.

"Almost there, sweet pea," she said as brightly as she could manage. They were only a few minutes out of Frederick now, and early for the appointment for once.

She glanced in the rearview mirror. She couldn't see the pickup anymore.

Frowning, she looked forward, her gaze drawn to the green directional sign coming up fast on her right, informing her of an upcoming exit. It was a couple of exits before the one she'd planned to take, but the prickling skin on the back of her neck made the decision for her.

She moved to the exit lane as quickly as she could and took the off-ramp. As she came to a stop at the bottom of the off-ramp, she spotted the blue pickup driving past her, continuing on the highway.

Blowing out a pent-up breath, she couldn't hold back a soft bubble of laughter. Talk about jumping at shadows.

"Firsty," Katie announced from her car seat.

"I know you're thirsty, sweetie. As soon as we get to the employment office, I'll get your apple juice for you, okay?" Lacey wasn't sure how much her niece really understood at the age of two, but the little girl subsided into silence for the remainder of the slightly longer drive into Frederick.

Elite Employment Agency occupied a tall, narrow redbrick building near the end of a block of old restored row homes in the downtown area. To Lacey's chagrin, there were no parking slots available on the street, but a small sign in front of the office indicated there was more parking available in the alley behind the building.

Lacey tamped down a creeping sense of alarm and followed the sign until she reached a narrow alley flanked on either side by what looked like large, sprawling garages. At the time some of these homes had been built, she realized, these garages might have been stables for carriage horses. They'd obviously been updated once automobiles became ubiquitous, but there was a quaint feeling here among the garages, as if she could pull open one of the doors and find herself immersed in the remains of the town's rich history.

But as she parked in the small gravel lot behind the employment agency, some of the alley's charm faded, for she found herself hemmed in between two large garages on either side and also behind her, where garages for the buildings on the next street closed the alley in like a narrow gorge.

Sunlight struggled to penetrate the steel-gray winter sky overhead, reminding Lacey that snow was expected later in the week. She hoped the interview with the prospective nanny would go quickly and well. The sooner she could get a nanny hired and settled into the old farmhouse, the better.

"Firsty?" Katie ventured from the backseat as Lacey turned off the car.

"Just a second, baby." She reached across the seat for the diaper bag, praying she'd remembered to pack the apple juice. And extra diapers.

With relief, she found the cup of apple juice and snapped off the drinking-spout cover. "Here, sweetie."

Katie grabbed the cup and upended it, drinking with greedy sucking sounds. Lacey took advantage of her niece's preoccupation to gather up the bag and her purse. She checked twice to make sure she had the car keys before she got out and walked around to the trunk to retrieve Katie's stroller.

The crunch of gravel was the only warning she got. It was just enough for her to reach into the trunk before a pair of arms wrapped around her and started dragging her away from the car.

She fought to stay with the car, wrapping her fingers around the first thing they found—the cold metallic bite of a tire iron. As the arms around her tightened like a vise, she twisted to one side and swung the tire iron downward. It wasn't a solid hit, but the iron connected with her captor's leg, and she heard a loud bark of pain and a stream of profanities in her ear.

The arms around her loosened, just a bit, but it was enough for her to jerk out of his grasp. Her first instinct was to run as far and as fast as she could, but the sound of Katie's cries, muffled by the car windows, stopped her cold.

She swung around to face her captor, wielding the tire iron in front of her like a club. But whatever small bravado she could muster faltered as she saw the barrel of a large black pistol aimed straight for her heart. All of the earlier ambient noises of the day—the rustle of wind in the winter-bare trees, the hum of nearby traffic—were swallowed by the thunderous throb of her pulse in her ears. Her entire focus centered on the dark, black hole of the pistol's barrel and the masked man who wielded it.

"Hey!" A man's voice broke through the swoosh of blood in her ears, and the pistol barrel swung quickly away from her, aimed at the newcomer.

Jerking out of her frozen trance, she swung at the man as hard as she could, hitting his shoulder and sending him stumbling toward the alley. The pistol went flying under a nearby car as the man caught himself against its trunk. He pushed upright again, staring at Lacey for a moment, then at something down the alley.

"Stop!" The voice that had broken through her paralysis belonged to a tall, broad-shouldered man in a neat charcoal suit who was running toward the man in the mask. He was still several yards away but gaining ground.

The masked man bolted down the alley, moving fast for someone his size. The man in the suit tried to pick up speed, but his dress shoes slipped and slid across the slick surface of the alley, and the man who'd pulled the gun on Lacey outdistanced him easily. There was a green van waiting halfway down the alley. The man in the mask jumped into the passenger seat and the car sped down the alley, took a turn and drove quickly out of sight.

Lacey opened the back door of her car and unbuckled her sobbing niece from the car seat, pulling her close and murmuring soft words of comfort to her as the man in the suit returned to where she stood, giving her a look of apology.

"Are you okay?" he asked, stopping short as she backpedaled away from him. "You're not hurt, are you?"

She tucked Katie closer, keeping a wary eye on the newcomer. Just because he'd tried to come to her rescue didn't mean he was anyone she could trust. Especially not now.

"I'm fine."

He reached into his pocket slowly and withdrew a cell phone. He waggled it toward her as if to reassure her that it wasn't any sort of weapon. "I'll call the police."

She looked behind her, where the back door of the building posed an almost irresistible temptation. She didn't want to deal with the cops. She'd had her fill of the police in the past few weeks since her sister's death. She knew they were just doing their job. Intrusive questions and suspicious minds came with the territory. Her own line of work shared some of those pitfalls; the people she interviewed were often emotionally distraught or shattered by the events they'd witnessed.

But knowing those facts didn't make it easy to be on the other side of the interrogation. Especially when what was left of your sister and brother-in-law had just been zipped into body bags and carted off to the morgue.

"I don't remember anything about him," she murmured, feeling sick. Katie sniffled against her shoulder, but at least her wails had subsided.

"Not much to remember," her rescuer said gently. "Did you see where his weapon went?"

"Yes," she said quickly. "Under that car." She nodded toward the late-model Buick parked next to hers. "But don't try to retrieve it. He might have left trace evidence."

"I know." He punched numbers into the phone as he crouched beside the Buick and looked under the chassis. "A woman was just accosted by an armed man in the alley behind Elite Employment Agency on Sixth. No, nobody's injured. The man lost possession of his weapon. I'm looking at it right now."

Lacey's knees began to shake, and she had to lean against the side of her car. Katie began to feel like deadweight in her arms, and, to her horror, she felt herself losing her grip on the little girl.

"Whoa, now." The man rose quickly to his feet and caught Katie as she started to slide out of Lacey's arms. "I've got her."

Lacey waited for Katie's wails to start, but to her surprise, the little girl just stared up with bright, curious eyes at the man in the suit. Bracing herself against the side of the car, Lacey held out her arms. "I'm all right. I can take her back now."

He ignored her outstretched arms and opened the passenger door of her car. Nodding toward the seat, he said, "Why don't you sit down right there, and then I'll give this cutie back to you."

It was a good idea, so she sat sideways, her feet still on the pavement. The man handed Katie back to her, and the little girl wriggled around until she was facing the stranger.

Katie was smitten, Lacey realized with some surprise, glancing up at the man, who was still making funny faces at Katie. Now that she wasn't drowning in adrenaline, Lacey could see why. Their rescuer was a good-looking man, with a mobile face that seemed made for smiling. His exertions had mussed his short, sandy-brown hair, revealing a tendency to curl.

His gaze shifted away from Katie and settled on Lacey, warmth shining in his hazel-green eyes. Sympathy tinged his voice when he spoke. "Feeling a little less shaky?"

"Yes, thanks." The moan of sirens in the distance seeped through the sound of traffic noise. "That must be the cops."

"Must be." The man smiled faintly. "I'm Jim Mercer."

"I'm Lacey Miles."

His smile spread. "I know. I've seen you on TV."

"Oh." She still felt strange when people recognized her, even though she had just finished her third year on air with the news network. "I haven't thanked you. I don't know what I'd have done if you hadn't shown up and chased that creep away."

He glanced at the tire iron she'd dropped by the car. "Probably brained the guy," he said wryly.

She laughed, even though nothing about the past few minutes was funny.

The sirens grew louder, and the flash of blue and cherry lights lit the gloom of the alley. A second later, a white-and-blue Frederick Police Department cruiser pulled up behind Lacey's car.

The next half hour proved to be almost as stressful as the attempted ambush, as Lacey had to answer dozens of questions, first from the responding officers, then from the detective who arrived a few minutes later. Because of the cold, the detectives took them inside the employment-agency building to ask questions, but the warmer temperatures didn't do much to improve Katie's mood. She cried every time Lacey tried to put her in the stroller, so Lacey ended up answering the detective's questions while bouncing a fretful Katie on her knee.

"He was wearing a mask," Lacey answered for what felt like the tenth time. "I didn't see his hair or his eyes. He was pointing a gun at me. I just saw the gun."

At the other end of the conference-room table, Jim Mercer was answering questions posed by another detective, who looked bored and sleepy. Jim glanced her way once, his eyes soft with concern. A warm sensation spread through her chest in response, catching her off guard.

He's a stranger, and you are in no position to

feel anything for a stranger, she reminded herself. *Trust no one.*

Detective Braun finally closed his notebook and held out a business card. "We'll see if we can get anything off the weapon. But even if we can track it with the serial number, it's possible it was stolen. However, you can call me if you remember anything else, and I'll be in touch if we're able to track anything down on your assailant. It's just—"

"I understand." She took the card. "I know there's not much to go on."

"You might want to call a friend to drive back to Virginia with you," he suggested. "So you're not out there alone."

She nodded even though she knew there was nobody she could call. Her work had been the center of her life for the past ten years, to the point that it consumed her life almost entirely. The low pay and bad hours paying her dues on the local level, then the big move to the occasional national gig and, finally, a regular investigative slot on a national network—all those steps up the career ladder had taken a big toll on the rest of her life.

She'd always thought there would be time later, time to rebuild friendships and family ties that had suffered during her upward climb.

Now Katie was all she had left, and she had

absolutely no idea how to be a mother to her sister's child.

"Do you think it could be connected to the bombing?" she asked Braun as he started toward the conference-room door.

He stopped and looked at her. "It's possible. But this attack seems pretty random."

"Someone set a bomb in my car. My sister and her husband were killed because they borrowed it. Maybe you remember that bombing—Marianne and Toby Harper? Ring any bells? And now, two weeks later, I'm accosted at gunpoint. I'm not sure I'd call that random."

Braun looked both sympathetic and frustrated. "I don't know what to tell you, ma'am. You may be right. It may be connected. I plan to make a call to the DC police and compare notes with the lead detective in the bombing case. Maybe we can come up with a more solid connection."

As he left the room, Lacey tucked Katie closer, breathing in the warm scent of powder and baby shampoo. *Meanwhile*, she thought, *Katie and I are sitting ducks*.

"AND YOU'RE SURE you didn't make out anything about the license plates?" Detective Marty Ridge stifled a yawn.

"No," Jim answered, trying not to let his impatience show. If he'd seen a license plate, he'd have described it in detail. But the plate on the green Chevy van had been obscured with mud. Probably on purpose. He couldn't even be sure whether they were Maryland or Virginia plates.

"Well, we'll have to hope the weapon gives us something to go on," Ridge said in a tone that suggested Jim's testimony was going to be no help at all.

Jim stifled a grimace of annoyance and glanced down the table at Lacey Miles and her niece. The little girl was fussing despite her aunt's attempt to soothe her. From the expression on Lacey's face, she didn't know how to comfort the child, which made him wonder just how much she knew about taking care of a baby.

"Call if you think of anything else." Rising, Ridge handed Jim his card, but from the look on his face, it was something he did out of habit rather than any real hope that Jim could add anything to the investigation.

After Ridge left, Jim walked to where Lacey sat. Katie looked up at him and her pout turned into a smile. Something inside him melted as the little girl held out her arms to him.

"No, Katie. Mr. Mercer has to go now." The smile Lacey flashed in his direction was half-hearted at best.

"Actually, I have an appointment here. A job interview."

"Oh." Lacey's sandy brows lifted slightly as she looked him up and down. He quelled the urge to squirm a little at her scrutiny, even though her gaze seemed as sharp as that of any drill sergeant he'd ever faced during an inspection. "Well, good luck."

"Thanks." He left the room, his steps faltering briefly when Katie began to cry. As he closed the door behind him, he heard Lacey's soft murmurs of comfort, and he wondered if the little girl would be appeased.

At the front office, he gave his name to the receptionist, apologizing for being late and explaining the situation.

"You're lucky," the woman said with a friendly smile. "Your appointment is late, too."

He glanced back toward the conference room, where he'd left Lacey Miles and her little niece. "I know."

THE EMPLOYMENT OFFICE MANAGER was a tall, sharp-eyed brunette with the bone structure of a model named Ellen Taylor. She wore a sleek blue suit that fit her angular body to perfection, and her voice was inflectionless and polished. "I'm so sorry for your ordeal, Ms. Miles."

She spared a brief smile for Katie, but she was clearly not someone who had much experience with small children.

Join the club, Lacey thought. "I hate that I've kept the prospective nanny waiting."

"It's not a problem," Ellen assured her. "Are you ready?"

Lacey glanced at her own rumpled suit and Katie's tear-streaked face. She sighed. So much for a good first impression. "Sure."

"Good. Before we start, how do you want to handle this? Do you want me to sit in or do you want to handle the interview yourself?"

If she thought Ellen Taylor knew anything about babies or nannies, she might have asked her to stay. But she might as well go into this interview the way she'd continue after she hired someone—clueless and needy.

Besides, she was a professional reporter. She'd interviewed presidents, prime ministers and kings, as well as rebels and terrorists. If she couldn't handle asking a prospective nanny a few pointed questions, what kind of reporter was she?

"Very well. I'll let you handle it, and then when you're done, you can tell me whether you want to interview any other prospects." Ellen left the room in a faint cloud of Chanel No. 5.

"Oh, wait—" Lacey began, but the door had already clicked shut behind the woman. "Damn it."

She'd forgotten to ask for a résumé beforehand. She'd planned her early arrival so she could do a quick read through the potential nanny's employment history so she could ask intelligent questions. No reporter liked to go into an interview blind.

"Oh well," she murmured against Katie's cheek. "Guess we'll find out soon enough if we've found our own Mary Poppins."

There was a quiet knock on the conference-room door.

"Come in," Lacey said, taking a deep breath to calm her sudden rattle of nerves and pasting a smile on her face.

The door opened and Jim Mercer entered, a faint smile on his face. "Hello, again."

"Oh. It's you." Her smile faded. "Did you forget something?"

"Actually, no." He smiled at Katie, who reached out for him again. "Hey there, sweetie."

Lacey tugged her niece closer. "I hate to seem rude, considering how you came to our rescue, but I don't really have time to talk. I'm about to conduct a job interview."

Jim pulled out the chair across from her and sat. "I know. I'm the one you're interviewing."

Chapter Two

Lacey Miles stared at Jim a moment, her only reaction a slight narrowing of her eyes. Otherwise, she maintained a pretty impressive poker face. "I see."

When she said nothing more, he asked, "Is that a problem? Ms. Taylor said you had specified that you had no issues with hiring a male caretaker."

"I don't," she said bluntly in a tone that suggested just the opposite.

"You seem as if you've been blindsided."

Her lips curved in a faint, perfunctory smile. "I guess I have been, in a way. I didn't have a chance to look over your credentials or even get your name. I just wasn't expecting a man."

"Oh."

"I'm in a hurry to make a hire, you see," she added quickly, as if she realized what she'd just admitted made her sound ill prepared. "I haven't had much luck since I sent my request to Ellen. In fact, you're the first person who's even applied for the job."

He was pretty sure he knew why. The story about the car bomb that had been meant for her—the one that had killed her sister and brother-in-law instead—had made the national news. There weren't a lot of wannabe nannies willing to walk into a situation like that.

"Anyway, best-laid plans and all that." Lacey breathed a soft sigh. "So tell me about yourself."

"I'm thirty-four years old. I spent a decade in the Marine Corps, and then over the next four years, I went to college and earned a degree in early-childhood education."

"Really? First a Marine, now a nanny?" That piece of information seemed to pique her interest.

"I'd eventually like to run my own day-care center," he said, wondering if she'd believe it.

"What sort of experience with child care do you have?"

"I raised my younger siblings from the age of fifteen. My father was a police officer who died in the line of duty, and my mother had to go back to work. I had three younger siblings, ages two through eleven. I was their full-time caregiver until my mother remarried shortly after I turned eighteen. At that time, I joined the Marine Corps."

"That's your most recent child-care experience?"

"After college, I worked a couple of years as a nanny for a family in Kentucky." He slid his résumé across the table to her. "Their contact information is on my résumé."

She set Katie on the floor and picked up the paper. After a few minutes silently reading what was written there, she put the paper down and looked up at him, her gray eyes narrowed. "Assuming your references check out, how quickly can you start work?"

"As soon as you hire me."

"What about the family you were working for? You don't need to give them any notice?"

"No. Mrs. Beckett decided she was missing too much of her children's lives by working in an office, so she took a job that enables her to work from home. So I'm back in the job market."

"I see."

She fell silent again, her gaze wandering back to the résumé, as if she might find something new written in the words on the page. What was she looking for? Jim wondered. A reason to hire him?

Or a reason not to?

A tug on his pants leg drew his attention. Katie stood at his knee, her gray eyes gazing up at him with curiosity. When she saw him looking, her little face spread into a big grin.

"Hey there, Katiebug."

At the sound of his voice, she lifted her arms.

"May I?" He looked at Lacey for permission to pick up the child.

"Sure."

He picked up Katie and set her on his knee. She grew instantly intrigued by his blue-striped tie, her fingers playing with the fabric. He couldn't hold back a smile, which she returned with a giggle.

She was at a very cute age, just a shade past two. Pretty steady on her feet, starting to build her vocabulary, curious about everything that crossed her path—she had probably already started becoming a handful before her parents suddenly and tragically disappeared from her life, leaving her in the care of her aunt.

Her aunt, who was a single woman with a high-powered, very public career. Earlier, he'd wondered just how much Lacey Miles knew about taking care of a small child. He was becoming more and more certain she was clueless. No wonder she was desperate to hire a nanny.

"Katie likes you," she said. "A point in your favor."

"Ms. Taylor said you needed a live-in nanny. Does that mean you'll be going back to work soon?"

Lacey's sandy brow notched upward. "What makes you think I haven't been working?"

"I haven't seen you on air. I guess I shouldn't have assumed you weren't working behind the scenes." It wouldn't do for her to realize just how much he already knew about her. She was already on edge as it was, and the attack this afternoon had only made things worse for her.

It had been a brazen attack, during daylight and out in the open. Although, if he hadn't happened to be walking down that alley when he had, it might have been very easy for her attacker to kill her outright or carry her and the child away in the van that had been waiting for him.

The big question was why. Why had someone gone after her today? Why had someone set a bomb under her car a couple of weeks ago?

Just how much danger were she and her niece really in?

"I guess you know why I have custody of my niece now. I'm all she has. Both sets of grandparents are dead, and Toby didn't have any brothers or sisters."

He nodded. "I'm very sorry about your sister and your brother-in-law."

"They were killed in my car." She spoke as if she had to force the words from her lips. She was clearly dealing with some pretty hefty guilt about her sister's death. And he gave her points for being honest about the threat hanging over her head, too, even though it might be enough to scare a prospective nanny away in a heartbeat.

"If you're trying to tell me there might be a little danger involved in this job, I'd already gathered that much before I ever agreed to apply for the job."

Her sharp gaze met his. "And yet, here you are. Even after you had to chase away another attack on us just today."

"I did mention I was a Marine, didn't I?"

For the first time since they'd met, a genuine smile touched the edges of Lacey's lips. "You did."

"Danger doesn't impress me the way it might someone else."

"I'm not asking you to be a bodyguard," she said sharply. "I don't need a security detail. I think that would probably make things worse, not better."

He wasn't sure why she felt that way, but he

didn't want to start asking questions that would make her even more reluctant to hire him. "I'm just saying, I'm not afraid to work for you. If you think I'll suit your needs."

She gave him another long, sharp-eyed look. "You'd have to live with Katie and me at my late sister's farmhouse in Cherry Grove, Virginia. It's a small town about a forty-minute drive from here in Frederick. The house isn't completely renovated, but enough has been done for it to be a comfortable place to live." Her voice faded for a moment, and what was left of her faint smile disappeared completely, swallowed by a look of hard grief. "Marianne and Toby were hoping to have it finished by this summer, but they ran out of time."

Jim felt a dart of sympathy. "Were they living there when they died?"

Lacey shook her head. "No. Why?"

"I was just wondering why you choose to live there instead of in DC. I thought maybe it was to make things easier for Katie. Not wanting to take her away from the home she knows—"

"No, that's not it. Just the opposite, actually. See, I was keeping Katie at my apartment when… That night. Marianne and Toby were celebrating their wedding anniversary. New Year's Eve." Lacey's lip trembled briefly before she brought her emotions under control. "I don't want her watching my front door, waiting for them to come back and get her."

He looked over at Katie, who'd slid off his lap and wandered over to play with a stuffed cat hanging by a red ribbon from the push bar of her stroller. He felt a rush of sadness for the child, and also for her tough but grieving aunt. Neither of them had expected to be where they were, the only family either of them had left.

Both of them in danger they couldn't predict or easily prevent.

"I want the job if you want to hire me," he said flatly, meeting Lacey's gaze. "I think I can help you. And I need the work."

She didn't say anything for a long moment, and he began to worry that she was going to turn him down. It wouldn't be a complete disaster if she did so, he knew. There were other ways to accomplish what he wanted to do.

But it would be so much easier if she'd just give him the nanny job.

She rose slowly, still looking at him through cautious gray eyes. "I'll call your references today and see what they say. I'll be in touch, one way or the other. May I contact you directly?"

He rose, too. "My number is on the résumé."

She continued to look at him for a long, silent moment, as if trying to assess his character in that lengthy gaze. Finally, she extended her hand. "It was good to meet you, Mr. Mercer."

"Jim," he reminded her, taking her hand firmly in his.

She withdrew her hand. "Thank you again for your help this afternoon."

"I'm glad I was there. I'm sorry I wasn't able to catch the guy before he got away."

"Two against one isn't good odds. Even for a Marine."

He waited for her to gather up Katie and settle her in the stroller, noting the way her hands shook slightly when Katie started to whine at being confined again.

She needed his help. A lot. And not just with Katie.

He was counting on that fact.

IN NO BIG hurry to return to the isolation of the Cherry Grove farmhouse, Lacey detoured southeast to Arlington, calling Detective Bolling with the Arlington County Police Department Homicide/Robbery Unit. As lead investigator into the car bomb that had killed Marianne and Toby, he was certain to be interested in what had happened to her in Frederick earlier that day.

He met her in a small café a few blocks from

her apartment, smiling at Katie as they sat. "How's she doing?"

Lacey shrugged. "Hard to know. She's not a big talker yet."

Bolling gave her a look of sympathy before he went into business mode. He listened intently as she told him about the ambush in Frederick, copying the name of the Frederick detective who'd given her his card. "I'll give him a call. You sure you and the little one are okay?"

"Someone came to our rescue. Chased the guy away. There were two of them, did I mention that? The one who pulled the gun on me got into a van waiting for him down the alley from the employment agency."

Bolling frowned at that. "Sounds premeditated. Having a getaway vehicle in place."

"That's what I thought, too. I think they wanted to abduct me, Detective Bolling. Otherwise, why didn't he just shoot me right there?"

Bolling's brow furrowed as he considered that possibility. "That's a departure from a car bomb."

"Do you think the situations could be unrelated?"

"Maybe. But it doesn't seem likely, does it?" Bolling's frown deepened. "What were you doing at an employment agency in Frederick, anyway?"

"Hiring a nanny."

Bolling looked at Katie. "Does that mean you're going back to work?"

Why did everyone assume hiring a nanny equaled returning to her job at the network? What did they think—that all women just naturally knew how to care for a two-year-old when one was dropped in their laps?

Immediately, she felt guilty for the flash of irritation. Most women probably did have at least some clue how to care for a small child. Even those who weren't in the position financially and professionally to take a sabbatical from work.

"No, I'm not going back to work yet. But I don't have a lot of experience caring for a child." She stirred her glass of ginger ale with a long red straw, not meeting Bolling's gaze. She didn't want to know what he thought of that admission. Pity or disapproval would be equally unwelcome.

"Did you find a suitable candidate?"

"Maybe."

"If you'd like, we could run a background check before you hire her."

"Not necessary," she assured him. She was as capable as the police to run a background check on Jim Mercer. Maybe more so, since her network connections gave her access to information even the police couldn't get their hands on. Not without a warrant, anyway. "But I'd like to stay in the loop if you hear anything from the Frederick police about my assailant. I didn't get the feeling Detective Braun was interested in keeping me updated."

"I will tell you if anything important comes out of the investigation," Bolling promised. "You sure you don't want something to eat? My treat."

"No, but thanks." What she wanted, she realized with despair, was to go to her place in Virginia Square, sleep in her own bed and wake up to find everything that had happened in the past couple of weeks was nothing but a bad dream.

But that wasn't going to happen. Marianne was gone. She wasn't coming back. And Lacey couldn't shake the feeling that there might be worse yet to come.

"Have you given any more consideration to hiring private security?" Bolling asked.

"I've considered it. But I'm trying to stay off the press's radar, at least for now. Hiring security guards would just draw more attention to me." She lowered her voice to a whisper after looking around to see if anyone was listening. "Especially in Cherry Grove."

"You're afraid that instead of covering the story, you'll suddenly be the story?"

She nodded. "Katie has enough to deal with as it is. I don't want her little face plastered all over cable news for the next few weeks."

"You have enough to deal with, too. I get it." Bolling put a ten on the table between them and stood up. "Come on. I'll walk you to your car."

The temperature had dropped by several degrees while they were in the café, Lacey noted. The snow predicted for the end of the week might come sooner than expected. She'd have to make sure they were stocked with plenty of firewood in case the power to the farmhouse went out in the storm.

"Is this vehicle registered in your name?" Bolling asked as he helped her settle Katie in her car seat.

"No," she answered. "It belonged to Toby and Marianne, so I guess it belongs to Katie and me now. I might as well use it until I can get another vehicle."

"Just be careful, Lacey. Okay? I know it's possible what happened to you today was random, but..."

But it wasn't likely. She knew that already.

"I'll be in touch," she promised.

Meanwhile, she had some background checking to do.

JIM HADN'T FIGURED on hearing from Lacey Miles for a few days. He knew she'd already talked to the references he'd provided on his résumé, but he was pretty sure she wouldn't have stopped there. He'd been watching her reporting for a few years now. He knew she was smart, prepared, resourceful and very, very thorough.

So it was with some surprise that he heard her voice on the phone shortly after lunchtime the day after the interview. "Mr. Mercer? This is Lacey Miles."

He put down the Glock he was cleaning and sat up straighter. "Ms. Miles. How's Katie? How are you, for that matter? Recovered from the attack?"

She didn't answer for a moment, as if his questions caught her off guard. "We're fine," she said after a couple of beats of silence. "Just fine. I'm calling about the job you interviewed for yesterday."

"Yes. Have you made a decision?"

"I have," she said, her voice a little stronger. "I'd like to hire you to care for my niece. Were you serious when you said you could go to work immediately?"

"Yes, I was."

"Then could you be here by four this afternoon? I have somewhere I need to go this evening. Somewhere I can't take Katie."

He frowned, not liking the sound of that. "You're not going out alone, are you?"

"I beg your pardon?"

Damn it. You're a nanny, not a Marine. Remember that. She's your boss, not someone you're protecting. "I'm sorry. You're right. I have no right to ask you such a question. I just— After the bombing and what happened to you yesterday...forget I asked. Yes, I can be there by dinnertime. I just need the address."

"Do you know how to get to Cherry Grove? East of Lovettsville, near the Potomac. There's a big fountain in the center of town. Shaped like a cherry." She couldn't quite keep a hint of laughter out of her voice. "Trust me, you can't miss it. If you'll stop at the gas station across the street from the fountain, just ask for the old Peabody farm. They'll tell you how to get here."

"Got it," he said. "I'll pack a bag and be there by four. Will that work?"

"Yes. Thank you. We'll give this a try and see how it goes." She hung up before he could say anything else.

He punched in a phone number and waited. He got an answer on the second ring. "It's Mercer."

"Any news?"

"Yeah. I'm headed to Cherry Grove. This evening. She's going out and needs me to watch Katie. Says we'll give this a try and see if it works out."

"It'll work out," the voice on the other end of the line said firmly. "You'll make it work out."

"Understood." He hung up the phone, picked up his Glock and started cleaning the weapon again.

Chapter Three

"What do you say, sweet pea?"

Katie gazed back at Lacey, her gray eyes bright with curiosity, as if she was trying to make sense of the question.

Lacey ruffled the baby's blond curls and laughed self-consciously. "It's okay, sweetie. If Aunt Lacey doesn't know whether she's done the right thing, she doesn't expect you to know."

"Wacey," Katie said solemnly.

Lacey picked her up and gave her a hug. Apparently not in the mood for a snuggle, Katie wriggled in her grasp, and Lacey set her down on the floor again with a sigh. "You sure know how to make a girl feel better about her mothering skills, Katie."

Katie flashed a lopsided grin and toddled off to the window, where she'd left her favorite stuffed cat sitting on the windowsill.

Lacey looked around the small front parlor,

feeling entirely overwhelmed. When she'd decided to move herself and Katie out here to Nowheresville, Virginia, she hadn't realized just how little of the farmhouse had been renovated. Half the sprawling old Folk Victorian house was still trapped in limbo, somewhere between demolition and reconstruction, and she had no idea how or when she'd be able to finish the work.

The contractor she'd hired to assess the status of the renovation had assured her that the foundation had been made sound, the roof was new and there were no safety hazards to worry about, although there had been some question about the safety of an underground tunnel the contractor had discovered in the basement, which was the only remaining part of the antebellum home that had burned to the ground a few years before the farmhouse had been built on its foundation.

But most of the upstairs rooms had yet to be repaired and painted. There was a whole bathroom in the master suite that had been completely gutted. And the sprawling kitchen at the back of the house was only halfway finished, though most of the remaining work was cosmetic rather than functional.

Poor Jim Mercer didn't have any idea what kind of mess he was about to walk into.

Her cell phone rang, a jarring note in the bucolic peace of the isolated farm. She checked the display and grimaced when she saw the name. "Hi, Royce."

"I heard you're hiring a nanny."

"Where'd you hear that?" she asked, wondering which employee of Elite Employment Agency had let that information slip to the wrong person.

"Oh, around. You know."

Maybe it had been Jim Mercer himself who'd spilled the news. Maybe he'd decided to do a little background checking on her, as well. She couldn't really blame him if he had, she realized. He had a right to know just what sort of mess he was walking into if he took the job. "You called to find out whether or not I'm hiring a nanny?"

"No," Royce said in a tone of long-suffering forbearance. "I called to find out whether your decision to hire a nanny meant you were coming back to work."

"Not yet. You said I could take a few months. Have you changed your mind?"

"If I said I had, would you come back to work?"

"No," she answered flatly. "I need this time off, Royce. If you can't give it to me, I'll turn in my notice. Then when I'm ready to return to work, I'll give one of the other networks a call."

"No," Royce said quickly. "I said you could have the sabbatical. I'm not going to renege."

"I really do appreciate your understanding."

"I hear the cops still don't know who set the bomb or why. Do you think it had something to do with that piece you were doing on al Adar?"

"I don't know," she admitted. Not long before the car bomb that had killed Marianne and Toby, Lacey had spent several months in Kaziristan, a Central Asian republic fighting for its very existence. A terrorist group known as al Adar had risen from the ashes earlier in the year, after several years of near dormancy, taking advantage of an economic downturn in the nascent democracy to stir up trouble and violence. Her exposé on the troubling rise of the terrorist group had just been nominated for a Murrow Award for investigative reporting.

But al Adar hadn't yet made a name for themselves outside of Kaziristan. They hadn't really started exporting terrorism on a regular basis, despite a few aborted attempts a few years back.

Or had they?

"I want to hire security for you and your niece."

"Royce, we've talked about this. If I make a big deal out of what happened, the press will do the same. They'll start publicizing where I am now, something that only a few people know about at the moment. Since I'd like to keep it that way, no—I'm not going to hire a bunch of bodyguards that'll start tongues wagging all over the East Coast."

"You're a target, Lacey."

"I've taken a sabbatical. I'm not reporting on al Adar or anyone else. Maybe that'll be enough to appease whoever it was who came after me." She wasn't sure she believed it, but the last thing she wanted right now was to live under the watchful eyes of a bunch of muscle-bound security contractors who'd try to watch her every move and keep her from doing what needed to be done.

Regardless of who had set the bomb under her car, she was the one who felt responsible for her sister's death.

She had to be the one who figured out who hated her enough to kill her. And stop him before he could take another shot at killing her.

"Do you really think it'll be enough to appease someone who wants you dead?" Royce asked.

"I don't know. But it's better than living in a cage until the cops finally figure out who set the bomb."

Royce was silent for a long moment before he spoke in a hushed tone. "Tell me you're not thinking about tracking down this killer yourself."

She didn't respond.

"Damn it, Lacey. You're a reporter. You're not a cop."

"I tracked down the head of al Adar when the US government thought the man was dead."

"Different situation. You weren't his target, for one thing."

There was a knock on the front door. "I have to go, Royce. I'll call you later."

She hung up the phone and walked to the front door, sneaking a peek through the security lens. Jim Mercer stood on the other side of the door, dressed in a brown leather bomber jacket, his hair ruffled by the cold wind moaning in the eaves outside.

She unlocked the door and opened it. "You're early."

His eyebrows lifted slightly. "Is that a problem?"

"No, of course not. I just mean, you're not late." She forced a smile, acutely aware that the past two weeks had done a number on her social skills. "Come in. I'll show you your room and you can get settled before I have to leave." She closed the door behind him, careful to lock the dead bolt.

He stopped in the middle of the foyer and looked around. "This place is great. How old is it?"

"I think it was built in the eighteen nineties. Something like that. It was updated in the sixties or seventies, I think, but Marianne and Toby were planning to renovate the place with its history in mind. You know, try to match the styles of the Folk Victorian era even while they updated the plumbing and electrical." She led him into the large family room. "They did take down a couple of walls to make this place more open concept, but the hardwood floors are all original, and so are the window trim and the crown molding."

"It's beautiful," he said.

Katie turned at the sound of his voice, staring at him with a look of sheer delight. "Hey!"

Jim grinned back at her. "Hey there, Katie-bug!"

She ran toward him, her chubby legs churning, and tugged on his jeans until he put down his duffel bag and picked her up. She patted his cheeks and again said, "Hey."

"She's usually so shy," Lacey murmured, not sure her niece's crush on her new nanny was such a good idea. What if Jim didn't work out? What if another person disappeared from Katie's life?

But what could she do? She needed help with her niece, someone to take care of the little girl while she continued her investigation into her sister's death. Better that it be someone Katie liked than someone she didn't, right?

Jim tucked Katie into the crook of one arm and picked up the duffel bag with the other. "Kids like me," he said with a shrug, nodding for her to continue the tour of the house.

She took him through the kitchen to the narrow hallway that led to the first-floor master bedroom. She had been staying there because it was close to the nursery, although for the past two weeks, Katie had been sleeping in the bed with Lacey.

She thought it might be better for her to move to one of the other bedrooms downstairs and let Jim have the bedroom suite. Katie could move to the nursery next door, and he'd still be close enough to go to her in the night.

"This is your room," she told him as she opened the door and led him inside.

He looked around the large room, his brow furrowed. "This is a nice room."

"It's technically the master suite, but it's next door to the nursery, so…"

He nodded, understanding. "You'll be upstairs?"

"No, the upstairs hasn't really been renovated yet. There are a couple of other bedrooms on the first floor. I'll take one of those."

"Of course. Whatever you want to do." He

turned to look at her. "How are you doing? After the ambush, I mean."

"I'm fine," she said with a firmness she didn't quite feel. Despite her determination to show no fear, the most recent attack had rattled her nerves almost as much as the car bombing had, despite the fact that neither she nor Katie had been hurt. Maybe because it had come out of the blue, in a place she hadn't expected to face danger. She had almost convinced herself that the bombing had been a onetime act of violent rage. A venting of hate and anger, perhaps, emptying a twisted soul of the unspeakable darkness inside him.

Much easier to deal with the idea of a psychotic outburst than to contemplate the idea that someone had deliberately set out to kill her in cold blood, driven not by emotion but rational if diabolical intent.

Jim set the duffel bag on the floor by the bed, bouncing Katie lightly in the crook of his arm. "I'll unpack after you get back home," he said, turning to look at Lacey. "Any idea how long you'll be out? So I know whether to start calling around to find you if you don't show up on time."

She couldn't decide if she found his words irritating or endearing. As she'd told Royce Myerson, she didn't want a bodyguard. She didn't want her movements tracked or to be trapped inside this farmhouse, afraid to stick her head out the door for fear of having it lopped off.

At the same time, she couldn't deny a sense of relief that she now had someone around who cared whether or not she came back home safely. Someone to call in the cavalry if things somehow went wrong.

"I should be home by eleven at the latest."

"If Katie and I need you, we can reach you by phone?"

"If it's an emergency."

"Listen, I know you're not looking for a bodyguard, and I don't imagine you care to tell a virtual stranger where you're going and who you're seeing, so I'm not going to ask you to tell me that." Katie had started wriggling in his arms, so Jim set her on the floor, not missing a beat. "But could you leave that information somewhere here in the house so that I can find it if you don't get back on time and I can't reach you?"

She narrowed her eyes. "You mean so the cops will have somewhere to start looking when you call it in?"

His brow furrowed. "Well, I hadn't planned to put it quite that bluntly."

She smiled. "It's a smart idea. I'll leave the

address where I'll be on the message board in the kitchen. Will that work?"

"That works." He returned her smile, and she felt an unexpected twisting sensation in the center of her chest. Damn, he was awfully cute when he smiled. She didn't need to start thinking about him as a tall, attractive man instead of her niece's nanny. Definitely needed to nip that in the bud.

"There are some jars of peas and carrots in the cabinet," she told him, leading him back to the kitchen. "And some creamed chicken in the fridge. She likes her food lukewarm. Not hot, not cold."

And she liked to throw her food around and make a mess, which Jim would find out soon enough.

"She's still eating food from jars?" he asked, sounding surprised.

"Marianne used to cook, and I think Katie was eating some regular table food, but I'm not quite that domestic," she admitted, guilt tugging at her chest. "I guess I'm going to have to buy a cookbook or something."

"I can cook," he said. "I don't mind."

"I don't expect you to be a housekeeper and chef, as well as a nanny."

"I like to cook. I like to eat. You'll be buying the groceries, so it's not like you'll be taking advantage." He crouched as Katie toddled up to him, smiling at the little girl. "We'll see if we can find the fixings to make a chicken pot-pie tonight. How does that sound, Katiebug?"

"Pie," she said in a tone of approval.

Damn it, Lacey thought. Great body, adorable dimples—and he cooked?

Even Mary Poppins couldn't touch that.

"Should I save you a plate? Or will you be eating out?"

"I was planning on grabbing something while I was out, but you're making this potpie sound tempting."

He slanted a smiling look at her. "Don't get too excited. We're talking about canned vegetables and crumbled-cracker topping here."

She really needed to get out of here before he tempted her to change her plans and stay. "Save me a plate. If I don't eat it tonight, I'll eat it tomorrow."

She grabbed her purse from one of the hooks in the small mudroom off the kitchen. "Don't start calling the police and hospitals until after ten," she said, keeping her tone light, even though she knew her safety wasn't really a laughing matter.

But she couldn't afford to live in fear. She had to find a killer before he struck again. She had to do it for Marianne and Toby. For her or-phaned niece.

For herself.

Outside, night had fallen completely, and the first grains of sleet peppered her windshield as she started Marianne's Chevrolet Impala. With Katie still small enough to fit easily into a car seat buckled to the sedan's backseat, Marianne and Toby hadn't yet seen the need to upgrade to an SUV or minivan. But it wouldn't be long before Lacey would have to start thinking about getting a more family friendly vehicle.

Stopping at the end of the long driveway, Lacey rubbed her temples, where the first signs of a headache were beginning to throb. How was she supposed to be Katie's mother? Katie had had a good mother. A great mother. A mother Lacey didn't have a hope of emulating. Marianne had been a natural. Chock-full of maternal instincts and glowing with the joy of motherhood.

And now she was gone, and all Katie had left were memories that would fade with time and an aunt who had no idea how to be a mother.

"Stop," she said aloud, gripping the steering wheel tightly in her clenched fists. "You'll learn what you need to know. You'll do your best."

And you'll start with finding the son of a bitch who killed Marianne and Toby.

A call had come early that morning from Ken Calvert, a source in the State Department, an analyst in the department's South and Central Asia division. She'd dealt with Calvert several times following up on the stateside elements of her investigative report on the rejuvenation of al Adar. Calvert claimed to have new information about a possible domestic al Adar connection, but he didn't feel comfortable telling her about it over the phone. He wanted to meet her at the Vietnam Veterans Memorial at seven.

Maybe she was crazy to go out there alone. But she needed to know if it was possible that al Adar had put out a hit on her here in the United States. At least the Vietnam Veterans Memorial was a public place. It might not draw hordes of tourists on a snowy night in January, but Lacey had never been to the sleek reflective memorial wall when there weren't plenty of visitors around. She should be safe enough.

She went east on River Road, heading for the highway that would take her into the capital. It was an hour's drive from Cherry Grove to DC. She hoped Ken Calvert really had come across something useful for her. She didn't look forward to driving home in the snow.

For the first third of the drive, traffic was moderate and, at times, light. But the closer she got to DC, the heavier it got. Headlights gleamed in her rearview mirror like long strands of Christmas lights stretching out along the highway behind her.

Any one of those vehicles could be carrying the man who had attacked her in Frederick, she thought. Or whoever had set the bomb in her car.

The thought that she might be sharing the road with a killer made her stomach tighten. She forced herself to take deep breaths past the sudden constriction in her chest.

Stay focused, she told herself. *Keep your eyes on the goal.*

It was a relief when she reached the outskirts of Dulles, Virginia, and the relentless darkness of the highway gave way to well-lit civilization. The endless stream of lights behind her became vehicles she could recognize—eighteen-wheeler trucks, expensive sports cars, sturdy SUVs and the occasional pickup truck.

Including a familiar-looking blue pickup just a few cars behind her.

Her heart skipping a beat, she checked her rearview mirror again to be certain.

It was the same truck she'd seen following her on the highway into Frederick yesterday.

She didn't like using her cell phone when she was driving. But she found herself reaching for the phone anyway. She shoved it into the dashboard holder and pulled up the farmhouse number on her contacts list. The phone rang twice before Jim Mercer answered, his deep voice instantly reassuring. "Hello?"

"Jim, it's Lacey Miles." She glanced at her mirror and saw the blue pickup keeping pace with her, staying a couple of vehicles back. Swallowing her fear, she forced the words past her lips. "I think I'm being followed."

Chapter Four

The fear in Lacey's voice caught Jim by surprise. She normally seemed so composed and competent that her shivery words made his chest tighten with alarm. "Tell me what's happening. What makes you think you're being followed?"

"The other day, before I got to the employment agency, I thought I saw a blue pickup truck following me. I left the highway early, and it passed on by, so I didn't think about it again. But the same truck is behind me right now."

"Are you sure it's the same truck?"

There was a brief pause. "I think it is." Her voice took on a sheepish tone. "I guess I'm not sure. It's dark out. Maybe I'm wrong about the color. I'm sorry. I'm probably overreacting."

"Where are you?"

"I just passed the exit to Dulles."

Dulles? She was nearly to DC. "I don't suppose you could cancel whatever you had going on tonight and come back here?"

There was a long pause on the other end of the line, and Jim realized the question was entirely inappropriate coming from a nanny she'd just hired that day on a probationary basis.

"I'm sure I'm overreacting," she repeated. "I shouldn't have called." She hung up without saying anything further.

Jim pressed his head against the wall, feeling stupid. He had to remember why she'd hired him. She was expecting him to take care of Katie, not protect her from whoever was trying to kill her. He couldn't come across as overprotective of her.

Katie looked up at him from her seat on the floor, where she was playing with brightly colored letter blocks. "Wacey?" she asked.

"Yeah, that was your aunt Lacey," he answered, settling himself on the floor in front of Katie, trying to decide what to do next. If he called Lacey back, she'd be suspicious. But what if that blue pickup really was following her? And why was she going to DC in the first place? A date? A meeting with the network?

Or had she been lured into a trap?

He bit back a curse, pulled his phone from his pocket and dialed Lacey's number.

She answered on the first ring. "What?" she

asked, her voice tight. He couldn't tell if she was worried or impatient. Maybe both.

"Look, I know you think you're overreacting, but at least stay on the phone with me until you get where you're going safely."

There was a long pause on the other end of the line. For a moment, he thought she'd hung up on him, but then she said, "The truck's still back there."

"Has it gotten any closer?"

"No. It hasn't turned off or fallen back, either."

"Wacey?" Katie queried, looking up at him with troubled gray eyes.

"Yes, Katiebug."

"Don't worry her," Lacey said quickly. "Kids can sense things."

"I know." He pasted a smile on his face until Katie's expression cleared and she went back to playing with her blocks. He spoke calmly into the phone. "I know you don't want to tell me where you're going—"

"I'm meeting someone at the Vietnam memorial."

He started to frown but froze his expression before Katie could pick up on his anxiety. "There's no parking near the memorial."

"I know. I'm going to park at my apartment in Arlington and take a cab into the city." She released a soft sigh. "I thought it would be safe. There are always tourists at the memorial. A wide-open public place."

"Maybe not in this weather. And you have to get there first."

"I know. I should have thought it through more." She sounded angry, but Jim knew it was self-directed. "I'm not used to being afraid of my shadow. I don't want to get used to it."

"Maybe you should call and reschedule whatever this meeting is."

"I can't. It might be something I need to know."

Jim lowered his voice, even though Katie didn't seem to be listening to him any longer. "About the bomb?"

"I don't know. Maybe about the bomb. I got a message from one of my State Department contacts. Said he had some information I could use. I didn't get the details, but I've dealt with this person before. He's been reliable."

"Was meeting at the war memorial his idea or yours?"

"His."

"And you're sure you can trust this guy?"

"I'm not sure about anything right now," Lacey answered, her voice taut with frustration. "Sometimes I think my whole life has been turned upside down and I don't know where to go or whom to trust."

Anything he could say in answer to that lament would probably make her suspicious, he knew. So he fell silent a moment, waiting for her to speak.

Finally, she said, "I'm in Arlington now. I should be at my apartment in a couple of minutes."

"Is your parking place outside or in a garage?"

"Private garage. Lots of security. I should be okay until I leave the garage."

"You want me to hang up so you can call a cab?"

"No. I'm going to go up to my apartment. I need to grab a few things anyway. That's why I left an hour early. I can call the cab from my landline. Listen, I'm at the garage entrance. I always lose cell coverage in the garage, so I'm going to hang up. I'll call you back in five minutes, when I get to my apartment."

"Be careful," he said softly, smiling at Katie, who had looked up sharply at his words.

"Five minutes," she said and ended the call.

"Five minutes, Katiebug. We can handle waiting five minutes, can't we?"

Katie gazed back at him, her expression troubled.

He held out his hands, and she pushed to her

feet and toddled into his arms. He hugged her close, breathing in the sweet baby smell of her, and settled his gaze on the mantel clock.

Five minutes.

THERE HAD BEEN a time when her apartment had been nothing short of a sanctuary. It was her home base, the place where the craziness of the world she traveled as part of her career couldn't touch her. Here, she was just Lacey Miles, sister and aunt. Good neighbor and, when she could find time to socialize, a halfway decent friend and girlfriend.

Until the night Marianne and Toby had died.

Just a couple of days ago, she remembered, she'd wanted nothing more desperately than to come home to this condo and try to recapture that sense of safety and calm. But as she walked through the apartment, listening to the silence enveloping her, she felt as if she'd walked into a strange world she'd never seen before.

Furniture she'd spent weeks shopping for looked alien to her, possessions that belonged to a different person from a different time. The vibrant abstract painting on the wall she'd found in a little art studio a few blocks away seemed lifeless, stripped of its beauty and meaning.

She pushed the thought aside and headed to her bedroom. When she'd moved into the farmhouse, it had been an impulsive choice. An attempt at escaping reality, if she was brutally honest with herself. The apartment was a vivid reminder of that night, of the phone call and the police visit that had shattered her life. She'd packed in haste, almost frantic to get out of this place, away from those memories. The farmhouse was a connection to her sister, but one without any memories to haunt her. She'd never even been there. Marianne and Toby had still been living in the city when the bombing happened. The farmhouse had still been a project, not a home.

Surveying the contents of her closet, she looked past the sleek, vividly colored dresses she wore on air. They had no place in her life at the moment. Pushing them to one side, she selected several sweaters and coats, the fleece-lined outerwear that she'd need, since the weather forecasters were predicting a snowy late winter. Rolling them up, she packed them in a medium-sized suitcase and set the bag by the front door so she wouldn't forget it.

She picked up the phone sitting on an antique cherry table by the door and called for a cab. A car would be there in ten minutes, the cab company promised. It would make her a few minutes late for her meeting with Ken Calvert, she realized, but it couldn't be helped. Meanwhile, it gave her time to pack the bag in her car for the trip home.

She was halfway down to the garage when she realized she hadn't called the nanny back.

Jim Mercer answered on the first ring, his voice tight with tension. "Is something wrong?"

"No," she said quickly, surprised by his tone.

"You were in the garage a long time. Longer than five minutes."

"I got busy. I packed a few things I'm going to need at the farm and I had to call a cab." She felt guilty, which was ridiculous. The man was her nanny, not her keeper. Why did she feel the need to explain herself to him? "I think you may be right. That truck was probably just headed to town like I was."

"I'd still feel better if you stayed on the phone until you reach the memorial."

"I'd feel better if you were concentrating on Katie."

"She's right here," Jim said. "We ate while we were waiting for your call. Now she's half-asleep in her high chair."

"Did she make a mess with her food?"

"No more than the average two-year-old. I'll clean her up before I put her to bed."

Lacey felt a quiver of envy. Most of the time, she felt completely out of her element with Katie, but the one thing both of them enjoyed was that brief time between dinner and bedtime, when Katie was drowsy and at her sweetest. She loved bedtime stories, and Lacey loved telling them. They'd cuddle in the rocking chair in Katie's pretty yellow nursery while Lacey spun the familiar old tales of princesses and evil queens, wicked wolves and hapless pigs, evil old crones and two hungry children lost in the woods.

"Give her a kiss for me." She reached the elevator to the garage. "I'm about to lose my connection again. I'm heading to the garage to put my bag in the car so I don't forget it."

"I'll get Katie cleaned up and in bed while I'm waiting for your call back." Jim's voice was firm.

"I think we need to have a talk about who's the boss and who's the nanny," she muttered.

"You were attacked a couple of days ago, and now you think you're being followed by the same blue truck that followed you that day. On top of what happened to your sister—" Jim's voice cut off abruptly. "I'm sorry."

"You said the guy who attacked me drove off in a van."

"He was the passenger in the van. But when he attacked, he came from the opposite direction, right?"

"Yeah."

"Maybe he had the blue truck parked nearby."

As much as she wanted to talk herself into believing she was letting her imagination run away with her, Jim had a point. "Okay, okay. I'll call you back. All right? But I've got to go down to the parking garage now, or I'll miss my cab." She hung up the phone and shoved it into her pocket.

A woman exited the elevator when it opened. She looked up in surprise at Lacey, her expression shifting in the now-familiar pattern of recognition, dismay and pity. The woman smiled warily at Lacey as they passed each other, and for a moment Lacey feared her neighbor was going to express some sort of awkwardly worded sympathy, but the elevator door closed before either of them could speak, and she relaxed back against the wall of the lift, glad to have dodged another in a long line of uncomfortable moments.

Nobody knew how to express condolences for Lacey's bereavement. Lacey herself would have been at a loss for the right words. How do you say *I'm sorry your sister was murdered in your place* without making everything a whole lot worse?

She stashed her suitcase in the trunk of her sister's Impala and took the elevator back to the lobby to wait for the cab to arrive. As promised, she dialed her home number. Jim answered immediately, his voice slightly muffled by a soft swishing sound Lacey couldn't quite make out. "Thanks for calling me back. I know you think I'm overstepping my bounds."

Surprised by his apology, she bit back a smile. "I know you're just concerned for my safety."

"But you're a smart, resourceful woman who's made her way through war zones. I know you know how to take care of yourself." A touch of humor tinted his voice. "I mean, I saw you with that tire iron the other day."

She released a huff of laughter, some of her tension dispelling. "Still, it doesn't hurt to have someone out there watching your back, right? Even if it's over the phone."

"When's the cab supposed to arrive?"

She glanced at her watch. "Should be anytime now. How's Katie?"

"I got about three pages into *Goodnight Moon* before she fell asleep. I'm just washing up from dinner now."

That explained the swishing sound. It was the water running in the sink. "You know, we have a dishwasher."

"I know. But when I'm worried, I like to keep my hands busy."

"I thought you knew you didn't have to worry

about me." She looked up as lights flashed across the lobby glass. Probably her cab arriving.

"Knowing you can take care of yourself is not the same thing as not worrying about your safety," he murmured in a low, raspy tone that sent a ripple of animal awareness darting up her spine. It had been a while since anyone outside of Marianne had really worried about her safety, she realized. Her bosses at the network wouldn't have been happy for her to be killed on assignment, of course, but she knew it was more about liability and the loss of a company asset than about her as a person.

Maybe Jim's concern for her was more about not wanting to lose his new job almost as soon as he'd gotten started. But something in his voice suggested his worry for her was more personal than pragmatic.

And while her head said there was something not quite right about his instant preoccupation with the danger she was in, she couldn't quell the sense of relief she felt knowing there was someone who cared if she lived or died, whatever his motivation might be.

The lights she'd seen moved closer, and she reached to open the lobby door as they slowed in front of the building.

Until she realized the lights belonged to a familiar blue pickup truck.

She froze, her breath caught in her throat.

She must have made some sort of noise, for Jim's voice rose on the other end of the line. "What's happening?"

"The blue pickup truck is in front of my building," she answered, slowly retreating from the door until her back flattened against the wall.

"Is it stopping?"

The pickup slowed almost to a halt, then began to move again, moving out of sight. Lacey released a soft hiss of breath. "No. It almost did, then it drove on."

"Lacey, you can't go meet your friend out there tonight. You need to get in your car and come home." Jim's tone rang with authority, reminding her that he'd spent a lot of years in the Marine Corps. She could almost picture him in fatigues, his hair cut high and tight, his voice barking instructions in the same "don't mess with me" tone he was using now. "Call him and cancel."

She wanted to argue, but he was right. Whatever Ken Calvert wanted to tell her could wait for another night. "Okay. I'll call him right now. I'll call you back when I'm on the road."

She hung up and dialed the cab company first, canceling the cab. "I have an account," she told the dispatcher when he balked at canceling the cab when it was nearly to her apartment. "Bill me for it."

Then she phoned Ken Calvert on her way back to the elevators. After four rings, his voice mail picked up.

"Ken, it's Lacey. I can't make it tonight. Call me tomorrow and we'll reschedule." She hung up the phone and entered the elevator, trying to calm her rattling nerves.

The walk from the elevator to the Impala was a nightmare, as she found herself spooked by the normal noises of cooling engines and the muted traffic sounds from outside the garage. She didn't start to relax until she was safely back on the road out of town.

Settling her phone in the hands-free cradle, she called Jim. "I'm on my way home."

"Stay on the line," he said.

"I'm feeling like an idiot right about now," she admitted. "Jumping at shadows."

"You're being safe," he corrected her firmly. "It's not like the danger isn't real, right?"

"Can we talk about something else?" she asked, trying to control a sudden case of the shivers. She turned the heat up to high, wishing she'd donned one of the heavy coats she'd packed before she got behind the wheel of the car.

"Sure. I could read to you. After all, I know where to find a copy of *Goodnight Moon*."

"That'll put me to sleep." She didn't know if it was the blast of heat coming from the vents or Jim Mercer's warm, comforting voice doing the job, but the shivers had already begun to subside. In their place, a creeping lethargy was starting to take hold, making her limbs feel heavy. "Don't you have any salty tales from your time in the military? Tell me one."

He told her several, with the seductive cadence and natural delivery of a born storyteller. Katie was going to love him, Lacey thought. Her little niece was a sucker for a well-told story.

The drive home seemed to pass in no time, unmarred by any further sightings of the blue pickup. As she drove through the tiny town of Cherry Grove, the snow that had been threatening all day finally started to fall, first in a mixture with tiny pebbles of sleet, then as fat, wet clumps as she turned into the long driveway to the farmhouse. "I'm here," she said into the phone.

"I know. See you in a minute." Jim hung up the phone.

The outside lights were on, casting brightness across the gravel drive. The front door opened as she walked around to the Impala's trunk to retrieve her suitcase. By the time she hauled it out, Jim Mercer stood beside her, tall and broad shouldered, a wall of heat in the frigid night air.

He took the suitcase from her numb fingers. "You okay?" he asked.

"I'm fine," she answered, almost believing it.

He followed her inside, waiting next to her while she engaged the dead bolt on the front door. "I heated up the potpie. I thought you might be hungry."

She was, she realized. "Starving."

He set the suitcase on the floor in the living room and led her into the kitchen, where a warm, savory aroma set her stomach rumbling. "It's not much," he warned. "Canned vegetables, canned chicken and canned cream-of-mushroom soup."

"Beats ramen." She shot him a quick grin as he waved her into one of the seats at the kitchen table and retrieved a plate of casserole from the microwave. It was warm and surprisingly tasty for something straight out of a can. "Not bad."

"I'm glad you're home safe," Jim said. The warmth in his voice and the intense focus of his gaze sent a ripple of pleasure skating along her spine. She quelled the sensation with ruthless determination.

He was Katie's nanny. Nothing more.

"Why don't you try to relax?" he suggested

when she started to carry her empty plate to the dishwasher. "I'll clean up."

"That's not your job, you know—" The ring of her cell phone interrupted. With a grimace, she checked the number, frowning at the display. It had a DC area code, but there was no name attached. She briefly considered letting it go to voice mail before curiosity made her pick up. "Hello?"

"Lacey Miles?" the voice on the other end asked. It was a male voice, deep and no-nonsense.

"This is Lacey," she answered, troubled by something she heard in the man's voice.

"This is Detective Miller with the Metropolitan Police Department. Did you place a phone call to a Ken Calvert earlier this evening, telling him you couldn't meet him?"

She tightened her grip on the phone and dropped into the chair she'd just vacated. Jim paused on his way to the sink, turning to give her a worried look. "How did you know that?" she asked Detective Miller.

There was a brief pause on the other end of the line. "We found the message on Mr. Calvert's phone. I regret to inform you that Mr. Calvert died earlier tonight."

Chapter Five

Lacey's face had gone pale, and her gray eyes flicked up to meet Jim's. Whatever she'd just heard over the phone had been a gut punch. "What happened?"

Jim eased quietly away from the sink and sat in the chair across the table from her, trying to guess the other end of the phone conversation by reading Lacey's expression. But she had recovered quickly from the shock of whatever she'd just been told over the phone and now sat composed and quiet, only a faint flicker of emotion in her eyes betraying her inner turmoil.

"I see," she said a moment later. "Of course. You want to see me tonight?"

Jim glanced at the clock on the wall over the table. It was eight-thirty. If someone was planning to meet with Lacey this late in the evening, something pretty significant must have happened.

But what?

"I'll be here," Lacey said finally before she ended the call and set her cell phone on the table in front of her, looking at it for a moment as if it was a dangerous beast she expected to strike.

"Are you okay?" Jim asked.

She looked up at him. "The man I was supposed to meet tonight was murdered."

Jim's gut tightened. "My God."

"He was found at a parking deck on Virginia Avenue, near the memorial, shortly after seven." She passed a hand over her eyes. "The police didn't give me any details, really. But a detective wants to talk to me tonight. Since I was the last person to call Ken on his cell phone."

"I'm sorry about your friend."

She shook her head as if to ward off his sympathy. "It wasn't like we were close. He was a source for some stories I did in the past."

"He had a new tip or something? Is that why he wanted to meet you tonight?" Jim tried not to sound too eager for her answer.

"Something like that," she answered vaguely, sounding distracted.

"Can I do anything to help you?"

She shook her head. "I don't know that I'm going to be able to add anything of use to the police. Ken was pretty vague about what he wanted to tell me."

And she was being pretty vague herself, Jim thought. It was too soon in their relationship for her to share anything personal. He'd helped her escape an ambush, which was probably why she'd hired him so quickly, but her gratitude went only so far.

He wasn't here to uncover all her secrets, he reminded himself. But his curiosity gnawed at him like a ravenous beast.

"You don't have to stick around for this," she said suddenly, pushing to her feet. "You can go read or watch TV or something. Go on. I'll be fine."

"I don't mind keeping you company if you don't mind," he said. "And if the cops start to suspect you of murder, I'm your best alibi, since I was on the phone with you for most of your drive time."

She slanted a look at him, a smile hovering near her lips. "You may have a point."

He followed her into the parlor, where she sat in an oversize armchair, tucking her legs under her. He took the chair opposite and tried to look relaxed, despite the adrenaline coursing through his body.

"Do you think the blue pickup truck has any connection to the murder?" he asked.

She frowned. "I guess it depends on when the

murder happened. I saw the truck in Arlington around six-thirty."

"Mr. Pickup Truck may have an accomplice."

She gave him a narrow-eyed look. "For a nanny, you're sounding a lot like a cop."

"Too much true-crime TV, I guess," he said with an easy smile. "And the whole Marine Corps thing."

"Right." Her expression seemed to relax, and Jim breathed a quiet sigh of relief. He was going to have to be careful with this one. She was far too observant. Part and parcel of her career as a reporter, he supposed.

They sat in silence for several long moments, the clock inexorably ticking away the time as they waited for the police detective's arrival. Finally Jim had all the silence he could stand. He pushed away from the table and rose. "I could use a cup of coffee. You?"

"Please."

He found the coffee in the cabinet over the coffeemaker and set a pot brewing. He took two mugs from a cabinet nearby and turned to look at her. "How do you like yours?"

"Creamy and sweet," she admitted with an almost sheepish smile.

"Nothing wrong with that," he said.

"It's hardly in keeping with my hard-boiled reporter reputation." She played her fingers around the edges of her phone. "Not much about my life now is in keeping with that, I suppose."

"Nothing wrong with that, either."

She crossed to where he stood, turning to lean against the counter next to him. "How did you do it? How did you transform yourself from Marine to nanny so easily?"

"Who said it was easy?"

"You're so good with Katie. It was almost instant. I've tried so hard to connect with her and sometimes I think she just barely tolerates me."

"Maybe you're trying too hard." He turned his head to look at her, and he was struck hard by the cool beauty of her. Cool, composed and untouchable, like porcelain under ice.

But there was a flicker of fire in those cool gray eyes that intrigued him, far more than he should have allowed, and it occurred to him that he had more to worry about than just Lacey Miles discovering his true purpose for being here.

"I don't know how to be a mother. My own mother died when I was ten, and Marianne only a couple of years older. I had never been one to play with dolls, the way Marianne had. She took to it so naturally, and to me it's such a mystery."

Against his better judgment, he reached out and touched her arm, almost surprised at its warmth. He'd been thinking of her as cool and untouchable, but she was neither.

"I wish you could teach me what to do," she said softly, turning toward him. He couldn't stop himself from facing her as well, closing the distance between them to scant inches.

A fierce tug of attraction roared through him, drawing him closer to her. Alarm bells clanged in his brain, but he found himself ignoring them.

Her eyes widened, but she didn't draw away, and he knew he was seconds away from a dreadful mistake. But he was damned if he knew how to stop himself from making it.

Rattling bangs on the front door made Lacey jump, and she turned toward the front of the house.

"Let me get it," Jim offered when she took a step forward.

"No," she said. "I'm sure it's Detective Miller. I'm perfectly capable of answering my own door."

He didn't argue, but he stayed in step with her, wishing he'd thought to wear his Glock. It was too far away if their late-night visitor proved to be a danger to Lacey.

The man at the door had cop written in every line and crease of his face, in the misshapen flatness of a once-broken nose and the cool suspicion gleaming in his dark brown eyes.

"Ms. Miles? I'm Detective Gerald Miller of the Metropolitan Police Department." He showed them his credentials. "May I come in?" Though his words were polite, his gravelly voice betrayed his assertive intentions.

He'd come in one way or another, no matter how Lacey answered.

"Of course." Lacey stepped back to allow him to enter and locked the door behind him. "Detective Miller, this is Jim Mercer. He's my niece's caregiver."

Miller's gaze coolly assessed him. "You're a nanny, eh?"

Jim didn't smile. "I am."

Miller's eyebrows notched upward, but he said nothing and turned back to Lacey. "I'd like to speak to you in private."

The last thing Jim wanted to do was leave Lacey alone with the detective, even though he didn't doubt that the man was exactly who he said he was. He'd seen his share of corruption among policemen and others in positions of legal authority. The badge was no promise of honor.

But Jim was in no position to make demands. He would be close should anything happen. He'd have to hope that was good enough.

"I LEFT THE message for Ken and drove back home." Lacey leveled her gaze on Detective Miller, waiting for his reaction to her story. He had listened without interrupting, which had surprised her. No doubt he'd have more than enough questions now to make up for the silence.

"What was it about the blue truck that worried you, Ms. Miles?"

"The fact that it had appeared to be following me. Not just this evening but also yesterday, just before I was ambushed in Frederick."

He nodded, but she didn't think it was any sort of confirmation of her words. "You spoke to which detective on the Frederick force?"

She had to think a moment to remember. Though only a day had passed since the ambush at the employment agency, it seemed almost a lifetime ago.

"Detective Braun," she answered. "I don't remember his first name, but he gave me his card. I think it's in my purse." She started to get up, but Detective Miller waved her back to the sofa.

"The last name should be enough," he said. "Did you tell him about the blue truck?"

"I didn't," she admitted. "At the time, it slipped my mind. I could write it off as a bit of paranoia on my part. You can imagine I've been jumping at shadows these days."

"I certainly can," Miller said in a tone that suggested he thought she might be jumping at shadows even now. Or did his tone suggest something else altogether? Perhaps he suspected she was using the tale of the mysterious blue truck to construct an alibi for herself.

Her heart sank. "I never spoke to Ken after his call this morning. When I called him this evening, I got his voice mail."

"We believe he was probably already dead by the time you called this evening."

"Do you consider me a suspect, Detective? Should I call my lawyer?"

"You're not under arrest. I haven't read you your Miranda rights."

"I'm not stupid, Detective."

"Is there anyone who can vouch for your story?"

She glanced toward the back of the house, where she could see Jim Mercer sitting at the kitchen table.

He looked up at her, his gaze intense.

"Jim Mercer can," she said, suddenly glad she'd made the decision to hire him.

"She stayed on the phone with me for the duration of the drive home. And she was on the phone with me for about a half hour before that, except for twice when she was in the parking garage of her apartment building. Apparently there's a cellular dead zone there."

"So she told you," Detective Miller said.

"Yes. I would think it would be simple enough to check her phone to see what cell towers the call pinged off."

Miller gave him a look of jaded amusement. "You'd think that, would you? You're a police officer, are you?"

"Fan of crime TV," Jim answered, letting his own jaded amusement show. "Look, Detective, I know you have a job to do. But I was on the phone with Ms. Miles tonight. I know she was worried about the truck following her. It was enough to make her cancel her meeting, the one she'd driven for an hour into town to make. I don't think she had time to do anything to Mr. Calvert, especially since I was on the phone with her for most of that time."

"It takes only a second to shoot a man."

"That's how he died? Gunshot?"

Miller's lips pressed into a tight line, as if he was annoyed with himself for having let that bit of information slip from his tongue. "I will check her phone records, as you so kindly suggested. And I believe I may ask a few questions about you as well, Mr. Mercer."

Jim kept his expression composed, but inside his chest, his heart jumped with alarm. His background had held up well enough to the employment agency's scrutiny, but if the police—or Lacey Miles herself, for that matter, with her access to a wide array of information-gathering resources—dug a little deeper into his background, they might find out that he was anything but a simple nanny.

Lacey came back into the front parlor, her posture straight and her expression cool and forbidding. "I believe we've both told you everything we know about the events of this evening, Detective. It's late, and I have a small niece who gets up very early in the morning. If you have any more questions, feel free to call tomorrow, but it's time to call it a night."

Miller's lips curved in the faintest of grim smiles. "I've heard you're a formidable woman, Ms. Miles. I've certainly seen your grit in action on my television screen. Your reputation was honestly earned, I believe."

She gave an almost regal nod, as if accepting his words as a compliment and nothing short of what she was due.

Damn, Jim thought. Formidable, indeed.

Lacey walked Detective Miller to the door and locked it behind him when he left. With a deep breath, she turned to look at Jim. Her earlier composure had slipped, and he saw worry lines creasing her forehead.

"Do you think there's a connection?" she asked.

He crossed to where she stood, shoving his

hands into the pockets of his jeans to keep from reaching out to touch her. "Between what happened to Ken Calvert tonight and what happened to you in Frederick the other day?"

"And what happened to Marianne and Toby."

"I don't know," he answered honestly. "What do you think?"

"I don't know, either." She moved away from the door, edging past him. He followed her into the kitchen, where she picked up a dishrag and began to clean the table. "I think that's what scares me. I don't know what any of this is about. If I did, maybe I could figure out what to do next."

He took the rag from her hand, surprised to feel her fingers tremble beneath his. She looked up at him, her eyes solemn and vulnerable.

The temptation to put his arms around her and hold her close to him was intense. He resisted it, but the effort left him feeling shaken. "I get the feeling you're not the type of woman who'd sit back and do nothing."

Her shoulders squared, and the vulnerability in her gaze hardened to steely resolve. "No, I'm not."

"Well, you don't have to do anything tonight," he said firmly, nodding toward the door to her bedroom. "Try to get some sleep. Maybe everything will make more sense in the morning."

"Maybe." She stepped away from him, and the warmth of her body fled, replaced by a wintry chill. He watched until she closed the bedroom door behind her, then sank onto one of the kitchen chairs.

He fished his cell phone from his pocket and dialed a number.

A voice answered after a single ring. "Roy's Auto Repair."

Jim answered with the code phrase. "I'm calling about my red Dodge Charger."

"What's the latest?" Alexander Quinn asked.

"Everything's gone straight to hell," Jim answered.

Chapter Six

The snow had ended before midnight, leaving a crusty dusting over the winter-dead grass. But the streets were clear, and the temperatures had risen above freezing by midmorning, leading Jim to suggest a trip into town to stock up on groceries.

"You know I didn't hire you to cook," Lacey protested mildly, more for the sake of appearances than for any real objection to his taking over some of the household duties. It would certainly free up more of her time to get to the truth about the recent attempts on her life. Besides, she had all the cooking skills of the average male college student, which meant she could manage a decent omelet and a pot of ramen, but not much else.

"I don't mind," he said. "What do you say, Katiebug? Want to go into town with me?"

"Go!" she answered with a grin, holding up her arms to him.

He picked her up and settled her on one hip, flashing a smile at Lacey that made her insides twist with inconvenient pleasure. "We'll be back in an hour or so. You can reimburse me for what we spend, okay?"

"Sure," she said, dragging her gaze away from his friendly smile.

"Anything you'd like me to pick up for you? Got a sweet tooth or an addiction to chips?"

She shook her head. "I'm not a picky eater. If it's edible, I'm fine."

"Okay. By the way, is there a spare car seat for Katie? I should put one in my car so we don't have to keep swapping back and forth."

"Yeah, there's one in the hall closet. I'll get it for you." She found the extra seat and took it back to the parlor. Jim was helping Katie into her coat and boots with enviable ease. "She's a lot more cooperative with you than she is with me."

"I have a way with the ladies," he joked, smiling up at her.

She couldn't argue with that, she thought wryly. "You want me to put the car seat in your car while you finish getting Katie ready?"

"That would be great." He fished his car keys from his pocket and handed them to her.

She grabbed her coat from the rack by the door and headed outside with the seat.

Jim drove a black Jeep Cherokee that looked to be a few years old. It looked neat and well cared for and had a leather and faint citrus scent. So besides being good-looking, a competent cook and great with kids, he was also tidy.

How the hell was this man still single?

The car seat fastened easily in the middle row of seats. She gave the seat a tug to be sure it was secure, then walked slowly up the flagstone walk to the front porch, where Jim and Katie had just emerged through the front door.

He took the keys from her, his warm fingers sliding over hers. She ground her teeth and allowed herself only a brief glance at him. "Be careful."

"I will," he promised.

"Call if you're going to be more than a couple of hours, okay?" she added. "So I won't worry."

"Of course." He touched her arm lightly. "Katie and I will be fine. But you should lock all the doors and windows until we get back, okay? So *I* won't worry."

"Will do." She eased past him, taking care not to let their bodies touch, and entered the warm house. She turned in the doorway, watching until Jim's SUV had reached the road at the end of the driveway. He made the turn toward town and she closed the door, pressing her forehead against the thick, weathered wood.

What was wrong with her? She hadn't had this kind of reaction to a man in years. Probably not since college.

It was embarrassing, really. She was a grown woman, near the top of her chosen field. She'd won awards and accolades for her hard-hitting journalism, earned the praise of world leaders and average citizens alike.

If anyone should be feeling flutters and shakes, it should be the nanny, not her, damn it.

She needed to get her mind on what was important. She needed to put those world-renowned journalistic skills to work on figuring out who was trying to kill her and why.

The second floor of the farmhouse still needed work, but one of the first things Lacey had done when she'd moved in with Katie was to clear out a small corner bedroom to use as her office. Morning sunshine flooded the room with both warmth and light, making it an ideal spot for her work.

Maybe, eventually, she would use it as her home office for her journalism work, but that wasn't how she was currently using it. Instead, it had become a sort of situation room, to use a political term. Here, she'd compiled every potential lead she'd been able to come up with in the days and now weeks following the car bombing.

If she'd ever made an enemy, his or her name was up on the big whiteboard she'd purchased and set up against one of the four walls. Her laptop and a Wi-Fi signal booster sat on an old desk she'd commandeered from the attic. It had been slightly rickety when she'd found it, but an old boyfriend of hers had been the handy sort, and she'd been interested enough in his woodworking hobby to learn a few things about furniture repair. She'd shored up the table enough that now it was as sturdy as the small desk she'd used whenever she worked from the news station.

She paused at the desk only long enough to check her email, which was different from the work account she used on her phone. Deleting the spam messages, she found only a couple of new emails. Both were from friends at the station, asking how she was doing.

She'd answer them later.

Moving to the whiteboard, she looked at the options she'd listed. There were eleven names, but most of those she could probably eliminate as people with grievances too petty to generate the sort of homicidal rage that would drive a person to set a car bomb.

She didn't kid herself that the bomb itself

would eliminate anybody on her list. The internet was full of sites explaining how to build an improvised explosive device, how to place it at the most advantageous place in the car to create maximum destruction and even the variety of ways to trigger the detonation.

Detective Bolling of the Arlington County Police hadn't shared the details of the bomb with her, but she had seen the gruesome aftermath of detonated IEDs during her time in the Middle East and Central Asia to be able to imagine the last seconds of her sister's life.

She forced those images to the back of her mind with ruthless ferocity and focused on the names on the whiteboard. After a few moments of consideration, she erased eight of the names, leaving the three potential enemies who best fit the profile of a homicide bomber.

Top of the list, based purely on their past methods of murder, was the rebel group al Adar. At the time of their inception during Kaziristan's move toward democracy, they'd claimed to have a religious impetus for their protests, stirring up anxiety and unrest among the country's conservative religious communities and throwing up roadblocks to the government's efforts at liberalization.

But after the group had taken the US and British embassies under siege nearly a decade ago, the group had transformed into a political entity that sought power and, along with it, control over the lucrative oil and natural gas resources of Kaziristan.

In concert with US, British and other Western allies, the democratic government of Kaziristan had solidified their position in the country, and al Adar had for a while been relegated to the sidelines.

But there had been rumblings over the past year or so that al Adar was trying to rebuild itself by taking a page from the playbook of ISIS, the Islamic State in Syria, and expanding their activities to other countries. There had been al Adar operatives discovered in Europe and Africa, and an email Lacey had received shortly before Marianne's death had come from an old, trusted informant in Kaziristan, who claimed that there were also al Adar sleeper cells in South and Central America, as well.

Could al Adar have already made its way into the United States?

Stupid question, she thought, using her dry-erase marker to draw a line under the words *al Adar* on the whiteboard. The United States would always be a target of any group wanting to make a name for itself.

She had meticulous files saved outlining al

Adar's power structure, operational tactics and purported goals. She would open those files and give them another read, see if she could find anything she'd missed that might give her greater insight into just what that group was capable of doing.

If al Adar was, indeed, involved, she had no doubt she'd be one of their primary targets for retribution, given the hours of news time she'd devoted to their operations over the years.

Unfortunately, al Adar was just one of the possible threats to her, based on her reporting.

Walking back to the whiteboard with a sigh, she moved on to the second possibility.

SMALL TOWNS WERE the same all over, Jim thought. Friendly on the outside, suspicious on the inside, at least until you'd proved yourself. The scrutiny had begun at the grocery store and continued when he'd stopped at the coffee shop on Main Street to grab a coffee for himself and apple juice for Katie.

The tall, broad-shouldered woman covering the front counter smiled at Katie. "Well, hello there, Miss Katie. Your usual this morning?" Her smile flickered down a notch when her brown eyes met Jim's. "Don't tell me you're the new nanny."

"Guilty as charged," he said, flashing her an easy smile. The badge on her blouse read Charlotte.

"Mind if I ask what Katie's usual is, Charlotte?"

"Apple juice," the woman responded, her smile still wary. "Can I get you something, as well?"

"Hot, strong coffee. One creamer, one sugar."

"For here or to go?"

"Sadly, to go. I have to get the groceries back before all the frozen food thaws." He added a touch of flirtation to his voice. "But I'll make sure I have time to sit a spell next time."

Charlotte's smile warmed up several degrees as she poured his coffee in a to-go cup. "You're a Southern boy, aren't you? We don't get near enough of those this far north in the state. I grew up in Roanoke, myself. I do so miss a good Southern drawl."

"I'm from High Point, North Carolina," he said, which wasn't the exact truth. High Point was just the closest town to the tiny mountain hamlet where he'd been born and raised.

Cooley Cove, North Carolina, wasn't on anybody's map.

"I have cousins down that way," Charlotte said, handing him the coffee and reaching into the cooler beneath the counter to retrieve a bottle of apple juice for Katie. "You got a sippy cup or something? I can pour it straight in for you."

Definitely warming up to him, he thought with a hidden smile. "That would be great. Thank you." He reached into the diaper bag slung over his shoulder and retrieved a clean cup with a sipper lid. As Charlotte poured half the bottle of apple juice into the cup, he took the opportunity to scan the small coffee shop, taking in the layout, as well as the handful of customers sitting at the tables and window booths around the room.

Five people. Two men, both over the age of sixty, and three women. Two mothers with children, who gave him curious looks, and an older woman sitting by herself in a corner booth, reading a novel.

No sign of a threat, and his Marine's sixth sense didn't raise his hackles.

"You enjoying working for Ms. Miles?" Charlotte asked as she handed the cup to Katie, who began drinking with greedy slurps.

"She's a nice lady," he answered carefully.

"A bit of a celebrity around here," she added. "Big-time reporter like her. Lots of people are curious."

Something about the tone of her voice pinged his radar. "People asking questions about her?"

She seemed to sense his sudden shift in intensity. "Oh, nothing bad. Just curious folks. It's not every day someone you see on TV moves into your little town, you know."

She was holding something back. Jim could tell. He lowered his voice conspiratorially. "I know *I'm* a little starstruck myself when she walks into the room."

Charlotte gave a soft chuckle. "She's a pretty thing—now, that's the honest truth. I suppose that's going to bring out the curiosity in some folks. That and..."

"The accident," he finished for her.

Charlotte's expression darkened. "That wasn't an accident. It was murder. Such a nice young couple, so looking forward to making their lives here. For such a thing to happen..." She shook her head. "What's this world coming to?"

"I guess you've probably had to drive off nosy reporters with a fire hose."

His dry comment was enough to make Charlotte smile a little. "Not quite, but there have been a few strangers coming through acting a little too curious about the Harpers and Ms. Miles for my liking."

"Anybody in particular? In case I need to watch out for them."

"Well, there was a fellow came through a couple of days ago, a stranger. Didn't bother with any hellos or how-do-you-dos, just got right to the point. He wanted to know more about what happened to the Harpers. He was asking if they had any enemies around here."

Pushy question, Jim thought, for some random passerby. "Could it have been a policeman?"

"I don't think so," Charlotte said with a shake of her head. "He'd have identified himself as such, wouldn't he?"

Almost certainly, Jim thought. The bluntness of the stranger's questions sounded more like an inept private investigator or maybe a young and hungry reporter, someone who didn't realize that a little schmoozing went a long way toward getting the information wanted. "Did you get his name?"

"He introduced himself as Mark, but he didn't give me a last name."

"Can I ask you to do something for me, Charlotte?" He reached into his pocket and pulled out a small business card. On one side was his name and cell-phone number. "If you see that man around here again, will you give me a call? I think Ms. Miles would like to know if someone's snooping around, trying to poke into her personal grief, you know?"

Charlotte took the card, giving Jim a solemn nod. "I'll do that. You bet I will. It's not right for people to come here trying to add to her problems. I'll definitely give you a call."

He gave her arm a light squeeze, then pulled a ten-dollar bill from the pocket of the diaper bag and laid it on the counter in front of her. "Thanks for the drinks and the conversation. I'm sure I'll be seeing you around."

He settled Katie in her car seat with her cup of apple juice and took a moment to look around him. Cherry Grove Diner was smack-dab in the middle of the town's small downtown district. Besides the diner, there were a couple of antiques stores situated across the street from each other, a small boutique that seemed to cater to teenagers and a small green park across the street from the tiny town hall.

It would be hard for a stranger to pass through town without people noticing, he thought. That was a plus.

But the farm where Lacey and Katie lived wasn't close to town. There was no police department in tiny Cherry Grove, only the county sheriff's department a couple of towns over. If trouble struck, he might be the only protection Lacey and her little niece had.

He climbed into the driver's seat of the Jeep, unease prickling the skin at the back of his neck. It would be all too easy for someone determined to do harm to accomplish his goals.

Picking up his phone, he called Lacey's cellphone number.

She answered on the second ring. "Everything okay?" she asked, sounding tense.

"Fine. We're on our way home."

"Okay. Great."

"Do you have a security system?"

There was a brief pause on the other end of the line. "No. I've been considering putting one in."

"I think you should," he said. "If you need a suggestion, I know a company that can put together a system to your exact requirements."

She sounded bemused. "Is that a service you've had need of before?"

"My previous employers used the same company for their security system," he answered. It wasn't a lie, though he left out the fact that his employer had, in fact, worked for Campbell Cove Security and had installed the system himself.

"I appreciate the suggestion," she said in a tone that suggested she didn't appreciate his interference at all. "But I have contacts of my own if I decide I need a security system."

"Of course," he said, making sure his tone of voice portrayed a contrition he didn't feel. "See you soon."

He ended the call and shoved the phone into

his pocket with a soft growl. The woman was being stubborn and hardheaded, determined to maintain her independence to the detriment of her own safety, and her niece's safety, as well.

Well, that was just too damn bad. Jim had come to Cherry Grove on a mission of his own, and he wasn't about to let Lacey Miles and her bloody contrarian streak get in his way.

Chapter Seven

After nearly a week of forecasts threatening heavy snowfall, the winter storm finally arrived, blustering into Cherry Grove midday on a gray Sunday and dumping nearly a foot of snow by the next morning.

For Lacey, the snowfall was nothing but an annoyance. There was too much snow for safe driving, and the county snowplows wouldn't make it out this far before the snow melted off. Jim offered to drive her into town in his four-wheel-drive Jeep if she needed anything, but the truth was, she didn't. She just didn't like feeling trapped.

Katie, on the other hand, seemed utterly delighted with the thick blanket of snow outside the farmhouse windows. Jim bundled her up and took her to the backyard, where they proceeded to construct a lopsided snowman with twigs for arms and coals from the barbecue on the back deck for eyes and mouth. Lacey dug a half-wilted carrot from the refrigerator's crisper for their use as a nose, and by the time they'd added Jim's baseball cap and Lacey's woolen scarf, the snowman looked almost respectable.

"Not a fan of the cold white stuff?" Jim asked as he settled on the back porch step next to her, his sharp gaze following Katie as she happily trudged through the snow.

"When you spend a winter in the mountains of Kaziristan…"

"Or Afghanistan," he added.

She turned her head to look at him. He was still watching Katie, but grim lines creased his face. "You did a tour of Afghanistan?"

"And Iraq."

"You spent a decade in the Marine Corps. Why did you decide not to re-up?"

He gave a shrug. "It wasn't the life I wanted anymore."

"And caring for children was?"

He looked at her, his gaze serious. "I enjoy it. I have a lot of experience with kids. I'm good at it."

She gave a slow nod. "Katie certainly responds well to you."

"Katie's easy. She's eager to make connections."

And yet, Lacey had yet to make a real connection with her niece. Katie always seemed tentative with her, as if she wasn't quite sure what she should do when Lacey was trying to interact with her.

"I could use some of your talent with kids," she murmured.

"Mind if I offer some advice?" He asked the question as if he expected her to say yes, she did mind.

She gave a wave of her gloved hand. "Offer away."

"Sometimes, the best communication is a hug. Or a touch." He looked at the little girl plunging through the snow with peals of delighted laughter. "Katie likes hugs. She likes to give them, too."

"To everyone but me."

"It's not about you, Lacey. You think you're doing something wrong, but to Katie, that nervousness and fear translates to her thinking she's the one who's doing something wrong. She wants to please you. The other day, when we went to the store in town, she talked about you constantly."

Lacey frowned, not sure she believed him. "She did?"

"Relax with her. Every interaction isn't a matter of grave importance. Let yourself enjoy her. You do like children, don't you?"

"I guess. I haven't really been around kids that much. Not in happy circumstances, anyway," she added, remembering some of the nightmarish scenes she'd witnessed during her time as a reporter in Central Asia. Being a child in a war zone was a deadly risk. The little ones were often the ones who suffered the most from man's depravity.

"Why don't you go play with Katie now?" Jim suggested. "In the meantime, I'll fix us some nice hot soup for lunch."

He stood and held his hand out to her. She took it, letting him pull her to her feet. As he started up the porch steps, she walked out into the snowy backyard to catch up with Katie.

The little girl looked up at her, a worried expression on her face. Lacey remembered Jim's advice and grinned down at her niece. "How's the snow, sweet pea? Cold enough for ya?"

Katie grinned up at her. "C-c-c-cold!" she agreed, reaching up one snow-packed mitten to Lacey.

Lacey dusted the snow off Katie's mitten and took her niece's small hand, nodding toward the snowman. "We need to give Mr. Snowman a name, don't you think? How about Marvin?"

"Mahbin?" Katie laughed. "Mahbin!"

"Marvin, it is." Lacey reached her hands down to her niece.

Katie practically threw herself into Lacey's arms, hugging her tightly when Lacey tugged her close.

A flood of emotion poured into Lacey, threatening to swamp her. She blinked back a swell of tears and buried her face in Katie's damp curls, wishing like hell that Marianne and Toby were still here for them both.

"She spends a lot of time upstairs," Jim said into the phone, using his free hand to spoon chicken and vegetable soup into three bowls to cool. "She keeps the door to one of the rooms upstairs locked, so I think that's probably where she goes. I haven't tried asking her about it, though."

"Probably best you don't." Alexander Quinn's tone was firm. "You're not there to poke into her business."

"I know." He lowered the heat on the stove, glancing toward the door to the mudroom. "But I can't shake the feeling that she's conducting her own investigation into her sister's murder."

"Can't blame her for that, can you?"

"No, but if she's going to be taking risks that way, it's going to make my job a whole lot more difficult."

"That's why you're paid the big bucks," Quinn said with a hint of humor in his voice.

The sound of footsteps in the mudroom off the kitchen gave Jim a moment's warning. "Gotta go." He ended the call and shoved his phone into his pocket, looking up with a smile as Lacey entered, Katie on her hip. Their noses and cheeks were red with cold, and Jim hurried them to the kitchen table. "You ladies look frozen."

Lacey set Katie in her high chair. "I think we're even colder than Marvin out there."

"Mahbin!" Katie echoed with a toothy grin.

"We named the snowman." Lacey pulled out the chair next to Katie's. "Please tell me that delicious soup I'm smelling is ready to serve."

"It is." Jim checked to be sure the soup wasn't too hot to eat, then set the bowls on the table in front of them. "I also toasted some French bread with butter to go with it. Would you like a slice?"

"My waistline says I shouldn't. But I think I will anyway." Lacey's wry grin transformed her normally solemn expression, shaving years off her age. Makeup-free, with cheeks reddened by the cold, she seemed barely out of her teens, though he knew from his research that she was thirty-two years old, only a couple of years younger than he was.

He set a slice of warm, butter-slathered French

bread on a napkin beside her soup bowl. "How about you, Katiebug?"

"Thpoon?" she asked.

He retrieved three spoons from a nearby drawer and passed them around, giving Katie the small one. Katie took it and dipped it into the soup, on the verge of making a mess.

"How about I help you with that?" Lacey suggested, taking the spoon from Katie's fist.

"I know it's messier, but maybe you should let her feed herself," Jim suggested.

Lacey paused with the spoon halfway to Katie's mouth and looked at him. "You think she's ready for that?"

Katie's mouth opened and closed like a hungry little bird, much to Jim's amusement. He quelled a laugh. "She's the right age to start learning how to use a spoon."

Lacey slowly put the spoon in Katie's bowl of soup. "Did you learn that sort of thing in college? What age they start feeding themselves? I feel so useless sometimes. Is there a book I should be reading?"

She looked so lost it drove all humor from Jim's mood. "You and Katie have been thrown together without any warning and, yeah, I could suggest a book or two, but honestly? Most of what you need to know you're only going to learn by trial and error."

Her eyes were bright with unshed tears when they met his gaze. "More error than anything else, I'm afraid."

"You had a good day with her today, didn't you? Out there with Marvin the Snowman?"

"Mahbin," Katie said around a spoonful of soup.

Lacey chuckled. "Yeah, we did."

"So, let's call that one a victory. Give yourself a pat on the back."

The look Lacey flashed in his direction was surprisingly full of vulnerability, and he realized just how over her head she felt in the role of instant mother.

He might have had other motives for taking this job as Katie's nanny, but he could also take some time out of his other activities to help Lacey learn to relax and enjoy taking care of her niece. He had been thrust into instant parenthood years ago, adopting the role of father to his younger siblings after his own father's death. It had been terrifying, learning how to parent by doing it because he'd had no other choice.

Katie had stopped eating and was now lazily drawing circles in what was left of the soup, big yawns and droopy eyelids signaling her need for an afternoon nap. "Katie, would you like me to read you a book?" he asked, unfastening her stained bib.

She nodded, reaching up for him.

"I'll clean up." Lacey watched them with a bemused smile.

After extracting Katie from the high chair, he took her into the bathroom for a quick washup, then carried her into her bedroom. She was still sleeping in a crib, though she was getting close to the age where she could handle sleeping in her own bed.

He settled in the rocking chair next to the crib, Katie on his lap, and looked through the reading choices. "What'll it be, Katiebug? Moons, brown bears or dirty dogs?"

"Doggy!"

Her enthusiasm suggested there might be a canine or two in Lacey's future. He wondered if she liked dogs.

He wouldn't mind having a dog or two. Especially if a gray-eyed heartbreaker was determined to have one.

He tucked Katie closer, picked up the book and started reading.

THE LOW RUMBLE of Jim's voice carried down the hall, soothing Lacey's nerves as she tucked her feet up under her on the sofa and checked her phone for messages. She had several texts from some of her friends in town, but most of them were quick check-ins she could deal with later.

There was a series of messages from her boss at the station, most trying to track down files and information that she could have found in a heartbeat if she were there. She texted back the answers and set the phone on the table beside her, leaning her head back against the sofa cushions and letting her eyes drift shut.

Had she been wrong to take the sabbatical from work? She had instant access to so much information at the office, plus plenty of face time with the handful of people who'd been with her in the war zones, both the literal ones across the globe and the figurative ones in the capital. They could help her work through her not quite coherent thoughts on the threats she faced.

Here at the farmhouse, all she had was a sleepy two-year-old and a nanny. Granted, the nanny was a former Marine, but was that enough to make him a decent sounding board?

What she needed to do was stop thinking. Just for a little while. All the stress she was putting on herself, on top of the natural stress of losing her sister and brother-in-law and gaining sole custody of her niece within the span of a few explosive seconds, was going to make her sick or crazy or both.

Shifting until she was lying on the sofa with her head on one of the sofa's throw pillows, she tried not to think of anything at all. But memories of her morning in the snow with Katie intruded, and they were so happy and carefree that she didn't fight them.

The air out here was so crisp and clean, a benefit of country living she'd never really considered before. She had never expected to feel the pull of the land itself, but it was starting to speak to her the way it had obviously spoken to Marianne and Toby when they'd decided to make Cherry Grove their home. The snow-covered fields stretched toward the mountains to the west, as pretty as a Christmas card.

Katie's peals of laughter had drawn her attention away from the distant beauty, focusing Lacey's attention on the pink-cheeked, laughing child.

She had no idea how much Katie understood about the loss of her parents, but Lacey was determined to make sure she always remembered them with love and peace.

Which meant she needed to forget her last sight of her sister, a wretched glimpse of charred body parts being gathered into a zippered body bag.

She tried to push that memory away, to let her drowsy thoughts drift back to the pristine memories of Katie and the snowman, but the dark night prevailed, an image streaked with blue and cherry lights from the vehicles of the first responders that cast the twisted metal remains of her car in stark relief.

No one could have survived that blast, but she had held on to hope until the final, stark image of the body bags. The police had tried to turn her away, but she had been determined to be there, to find out the truth.

The image remained so vivid in her mind it brought tears stinging to the backs of her eyes. The smell of charred flesh had lingered in her nose for days, long past the time it should have. It was a memory, not an odor. She knew that rationally, but even now, lying on her sofa, the smell memory filled her nose and invaded her lungs, making her feel as if she were suffocating.

She was in the moment again. Standing on the damp sidewalk a few yards from the incident scene. Crime scene, she corrected mentally, although she had clung to the idea of a terrible accident long past the time it should have been clear that what had happened to Marianne and Toby had been intentional. She was still thinking accident, still hoping maybe the police were wrong, that maybe in the explosion something had happened to the license plate that had made them read the plate number wrong.

But they hadn't been mistaken. And the desperate hope that the explosion had been a terrible accident had lingered only as long as it took for a crime-scene investigator to find the evidence of a detonator.

Surrounded by busy people trying to pull together the pieces of a deadly puzzle that had clearly been meant for Lacey herself, she'd felt separated from them, outside of time and space, as if she were floating somewhere near the scene like a wraith. Dead inside, yet still lingering in the world of the living.

She found that she remembered every detail of the scene, of the night itself, of the people moving about and the vehicles driving past the scene, heads twisted toward the destruction because nobody was incurious enough to drive past without looking.

She saw a limousine roll past, moving at a stately pace, but the black-tinted windows hid the occupants from view. Some senator, maybe. Or a high-ranking official in the Pentagon or at State. For a second, perhaps in need of a distraction, she thought about trying to read the license plate so she could later identify just which DC bigwig had slowed to get a better look at the evidence of her loss.

But what would that accomplish? The senator hadn't set the bomb that killed her sister. Nor had a general or a diplomat.

The only person responsible was Lacey herself. She had been the target. She'd pissed off someone or uncovered something that had earned her a death sentence.

A death sentence that Marianne and Toby had paid instead.

Lacey tried to drag herself out of what she now knew was a nightmare. All she had to do was wake up.

Just wake up.

She felt herself coming back to reality, but just as the dark dream started to disintegrate, she saw another vehicle drive slowly past the bomb scene.

A familiar blue pickup truck.

Lacey sat up with a jerk, her heart racing and her head pounding.

"Lacey?" Jim's voice was closer than she expected. She turned her head and found him crouched next to the fireplace, lighting kindling under the logs. He put down the lighter and rose to his feet, crossing quickly to her side. "Are you okay?"

"Just a dream," she said hoarsely.

"Looked like a nightmare."

She threaded her fingers through her hair, pushing it back from her face. Now that the dream had receded, her heart rate was approaching normal, and the throbbing behind her eyes had eased to a mild ache. "I was dreaming about the bombing."

He sat on the coffee table in front of her. "That's a nightmare, all right."

"I went to the scene not long after it happened. One of my reporter friends had learned from a cop that the license plate on the car was registered to me and had given me a call. Until I showed up at the scene, the police were going on the premise that I was one of the people inside the car."

Jim put his hand over hers, his touch gentle and undemanding. "I'm sorry. That must have been terrible for you, to see the wreckage."

"I saw a blue pickup truck that night," she said bluntly.

He leaned back slightly, dropping his hand away from hers. "You remember that?"

"Not until the dream."

He frowned, and she could see the skepticism in his eyes. "I'm not sure you can rely on what comes to you in a nightmare."

"It was real. I saw it. That night, the pickup drove by slowly, just like all the other rubber-neckers. He wanted to see what had happened." Her voice dipped lower. "Maybe he wanted to see his handiwork."

"You don't even know it's a man," Jim pointed

out reasonably. "And there are a lot of blue pick-ups out there—"

"It was the same truck. I'm sure it was. And do you know what that means?"

He shook his head slightly, but she saw the realization dawn in his expression.

"The police were filming the scene that night. Three-hundred-and-sixty degrees, to take in everything. I think maybe they had the thought that the bomber would want to see the fruits of his handiwork."

"So if the blue pickup was there…"

"It'll be on film," she finished for him, pushing to her feet. She looked down at him with a grim smile. "Maybe they were able to get the license plate. And if they did, I'm going to nail that son of a bitch to the wall."

Chapter Eight

It had taken Lacey most of the afternoon to get through to the detective leading the bombing task force, primarily because he and the other members of the team had been at a meeting in the White House, where the president's chief of staff had told them the investigation was moving too slowly. This information Lacey had learned not from the police but from her colleagues in the White House press corps. By the time she finally got through to Detective Bolling, it was close to six in the evening, and he sounded frazzled and surly.

"Do you have any idea how much footage you're talking about?" he asked Lacey when she asked about the blue pickup. "We took note of the vehicles that passed the scene and someone on the task force is going through license plates to see if there's anyone who matches our database of bomb makers. But that kind of thing takes a lot of time, and it's not the priority of our investigation, as you can imagine."

"So let me do it," Lacey said. "I can look at the footage and find the truck I'm talking about."

"If it was even there," Bolling muttered.

"It was there."

"Ms. Miles, you had a dream about the crime scene, and your mind probably conflated your more recent experiences with what you experienced that night—"

"Even if that's so, what would it hurt for me to look at the footage?"

"For one thing, it's police evidence, and we don't normally allow the press to view our evidence."

"I'm not the press. I'm the victim's sister. And I'm also apparently the real target of the bombing, even if it was my sister who was killed." Lacey looked up from her seat on the sofa to find Jim watching her from the kitchen entryway, his gaze warm with concern. An answering warmth flooded her body, and she forced herself to look away, not comfortable with how increasingly dependent on him she was becoming.

It would be bad enough if she was just relying on him for help with Katie, but the truth was, she was starting to need him just to keep herself from burrowing away from the world and obsessing on her sister's death.

"Look," Bolling said finally, his weary sigh a soft roar of wind over the phone. "This is what I can do. I'll talk to the head of the task force. If she agrees, I'll get someone to make me a copy of the footage, and I'll let you take a look. But it could be a couple of days."

"Can you ask today? And get someone to do the dubbing overnight?" she pressed. She glanced at Jim and saw his eyebrows lift at her insistent tone.

"That's asking a lot." Bolling sounded frustrated.

"I know it is. But the sooner I take a look, the sooner we'll know if this is a viable lead or not, right? If it is, you've got a new avenue of investigation. And if it isn't, you've eliminated said avenue of investigation."

And maybe she could discount all the blue-pickup sightings as a sign of her own paranoia.

"Fine. If Agent Montoya agrees, I can get someone on the night shift to dub the video and get you a set of DVDs."

"I can drive into town tomorrow to pick them up," she offered quickly, before he changed his mind.

When he spoke, his voice held a note of caution. "Ms. Miles, I don't even know if I'll get the go-ahead."

"Well, if you do…"

There was a brief pause before he said, "Well, I was planning to talk to some of your sister's neighbors tomorrow anyway. Just to rule out the possibility that she and your brother-in-law were the targets rather than you."

"They weren't," she said firmly.

"Nevertheless, questions have to be asked. I'll be in Cherry Grove in the morning. If I get the go-ahead, I'll give you a call and maybe I can meet you somewhere in town to hand over the DVDs."

"I'll buy you lunch for your trouble," she suggested, feeling a little guilty for pushing the detective so ruthlessly now that she'd accomplished her goal. "There's a good diner in town. Southern home cooking."

"You're just trying to make up for being such a pain in my backside, aren't you?" Bolling sounded amused. "I'll let you know."

"Thank you, Detective," she said sincerely. "I know it's asking a lot."

"Well, maybe it won't hurt to have fresh, motivated eyes on the evidence." Bolling's tone was grudging, but she could tell he was starting to see the benefit of her suggestion.

They said their goodbyes and she laid her

phone on the side table. "If he can get the head of the task force to agree, I might get the DVDs as early as tomorrow before lunch," she said to Jim, who was still standing in the doorway, watching her with that disconcerting gaze of his. She could almost feel it moving over her like a caress, which was a ridiculous notion, especially for someone as levelheaded as she was.

She prided herself on her rationality. Girlish crushes, especially on someone who was her employee, were not part of her repertoire.

"You want Katie and me to come with you?" Jim asked in a low rumble that made her shiver.

She squared her shoulders and shook her head. "It's just a drive into Cherry Grove. I'll call when I get there and call when I'm leaving, Mom."

His lips curved in a sheepish grin. "One of the pitfalls of being a nanny. Feeling the urgent need to take care of everybody, not just your charge."

"Sounds like something a Marine might say," she pointed out, allowing herself to smile.

"That, too," he agreed with a grin that made her insides twist with pleasure. "Katie should be up from her nap soon. I thought maybe we could do something fun for dinner. I bought some wieners and the fixings for s'mores. Hot dogs, marshmallows, chocolate and graham crackers—sounds nutritious to me."

She supposed she should be appalled by a dinner of junk food, but the thought of hot dogs and s'mores had her mouth watering. Katie had eaten healthy food for breakfast and lunch—why not do something a little decadent for dinner?

"Do we have any cabbage? I could make slaw so we don't go completely veggie-free," she suggested.

He flashed her that dangerous grin again. "I think I can come up with what you need." He headed into the kitchen and started gathering the makings of their dinner.

Lacey felt a disconcerting pull toward the kitchen, as if Jim were a magnet and she were steel. She pushed against that sensation, heading down the hall to Katie's room.

She was awake, drowsy eyes open and following the bird mobile over her crib. Marianne had confided in Lacey that she was dreading the day Katie outgrew her crib. "It'll be like she's not a baby anymore, and I'm not sure I'm ready for that," she'd told Lacey just a few days before the accident.

Toby, on the other hand, was happy to see his baby girl grow to the next phase of her development. "I feel like the baby years are all mommy time," he'd told Lacey with a rueful smile when Marianne was out of the room with Katie. "I'm looking forward to a little more daddy time."

Tears stung Lacey's eyes as Katie's gaze turned to meet hers and her niece's Cupid's-bow lips curved in a smile. She stood up in the crib and stretched her arms out. "Wacey."

Lacey lifted her out of the crib and hugged her tight, fighting to keep the angry tears from falling.

Now there'd be no more mommy or daddy time for Marianne and Toby, and it just wasn't right. Their deaths demanded justice.

Or maybe vengeance. Lacey wasn't sure which she wanted more.

DINNER HAD BEEN…STRANGE, Jim thought the next morning as he watched Lacey's car move slowly down the driveway. Katie had loved the adventure, watching with wide eyes and open mouth as Jim cooked first the wieners, then the marshmallows, over the fire in the parlor. But while Lacey had been all smiles and laughter, Jim had sensed that the show of gaiety was just that—a show. She was hiding her real feelings behind the smiles, and he got the sense what she was really feeling was bleak anger.

She had gotten a call from Detective Bolling shortly after breakfast. The bombing task force had called an unexpected meeting for early in the afternoon, which meant he had to be in Cherry Grove much earlier than he'd planned. Lunch wasn't a possibility, but he could grab a coffee midmorning and pass over the DVDs of the crime-scene videos.

It was a smaller window of time than Jim had hoped for, and it coincided with Katie's active time, but opportunities to snoop were few and far between. He wanted to know what Lacey was hiding behind the locked door on the second floor, and this was his best chance to find out.

He had never been one to let television be a babysitter, but at least PBS was educational, and Katie loved the morning block of programs.

He settled her in her favorite chair, gave her a sippy cup of apple juice and headed upstairs to the locked room, lock-pick tools tucked in the pocket of his jeans.

The doorknob lock was an easy pick, but at some point in the recent past, someone had put a dead bolt on the door, as well. Jim assumed it had been Lacey, since he doubted Toby and Marianne would have had any reason to do so.

But even the more complex lock proved to be no obstacle, and within a few minutes he entered the mysterious room.

There wasn't much there, he saw in a quick

sweep of the room, but what was there was…illuminating. A table, obviously acting as a desk, was occupied by Lacey's laptop computer, with paper files stacked neatly beside it. On the wall opposite the windows, she'd hung a whiteboard now filled with her neat writing.

This was Lacey's situation room, he thought. But there was no task force working out of this space. Just Lacey alone,

Pulling his phone from his pocket, he crossed to the whiteboard and started taking photos. He did the same with the files on the table, though a couple attempts to guess her laptop's password proved fruitless. He closed the laptop and looked around, feeling both queasy at his invasion of her privacy and deeply curious about what the whiteboard revealed.

There were three columns, separated by vertically drawn lines, with titles at the top.

Al Adar. Whittier Family. J.T. Swain.

Jim knew all about al Adar. He'd done a tour of duty in Kaziristan at the height of their power there. They were vicious and deadly. But their power in Kaziristan had been waning for years, and he had to admit that for the past few years, since he'd left the Marine Corps, he hadn't exactly been focusing on the life he'd left behind.

If anything, he'd been hiding from it all.

He couldn't afford that anymore, he thought

grimly. Not if al Adar was behind the bombing that had killed Katie's parents. He'd call Quinn and see just what information Campbell Cove Security had on the Kaziri terrorist group.

He'd heard of the Whittier family, as well. Everybody in America knew who Justin and Carson Whittier were. Handsome, charismatic and highly accomplished, the Whittiers were this generation's answer to the Kennedys. Their father and uncles had been highly successful stockbrokers who'd played the market with skill and ruthlessness during the volatile dot-com bubble. The sons were equally successful investing their money, and by the time they both ran for Congress from neighboring districts in Connecticut, they were multimillionaires in their own rights.

They were media darlings and, in the case of the unmarried younger brother, Carson, constant fodder for the tabloids. He was still in the "looking for his soul mate" phase of life, he liked to say. In the meantime, he was sampling all the fish in the sea.

With a Marine's inbred distrust of politicians, Jim had learned his life was far less stressful if he paid more attention to the things in his life he could control and less to the Machiavellian exploits of the political class, so he wasn't quite sure why the Whittiers would be on Lacey's list of suspects. There had been whispers of scandal that haunted any public figure, of course, but the Whittier brothers had managed to navigate those murky waters without getting any lasting mud on them.

Was it possible that Lacey knew something about them that, for legal reasons, she hadn't been able to report?

He didn't even recognize the last name—J.T. Swain. The name Swain sounded vaguely familiar, but he couldn't place it. Maybe he'd call Quinn and ask. If there was anybody who knew where all the bodies were buried, it was his boss at Campbell Cove Security.

With a glance at his watch, he saw he'd been in the room for under ten minutes, all the time he was willing to leave Katie on her own, even with the toddler gates blocking her exit from the small entertainment parlor.

He engaged the doorknob lock as he left the room, then took care with his lock-pick tools to relock the dead bolt without leaving any obvious pry marks. He disengaged the portable gates and settled on the sofa behind Katie, smiling back at her when she managed to drag her attention from the television screen long enough to flash him an adorable grin.

She was a real heartbreaker, he thought, acutely aware of the tug of affection he felt every time he looked at her. After playing father to his younger siblings, he had been determined never to have children of his own. They were too much responsibility. Too fragile for him to dare to love. His own brother and sisters he'd loved because they were his family, but the more they'd come to depend on him for everything they needed, the more aware he'd become of just how easily one or more of them could be snatched away from him.

This job as Katie's nanny was never supposed to be a long-term situation. He was supposed to come here, assess the situation, provide Lacey Miles with the protection she had refused to hire for herself, and once the police found out who had killed her sister and brother-in-law, he'd be out of here, showing up for duty back in Kentucky at Campbell Cove Academy, where he'd be teaching combat tactics for civilians and law enforcement to advanced students at the school.

He needed to put some emotional distance between himself and Katie and Lacey. It would be all too easy to let himself get so tangled up with them and the danger they were in that he wouldn't be able to easily find his way out.

Rubbing his forehead, where the first twinges of a tension headache were forming, he pulled out his phone and called Alexander Quinn. He quickly ran down Lacey's list of prime suspects.

"I get why al Adar is on the list," he said quietly, keeping an eye on Katie to make sure she wasn't paying attention, "but what do you know about the Whittiers or this J.T. Swain?"

"The Whittiers—I'm not sure. I'd have to poke around, call in a few favors and see if I could separate fiction from fact. But I know someone who could put you in touch with someone who knows a whole hell of a lot about J.T. Swain."

"Who is he?"

"He was a backwoods drug kingpin. Part of a family of redneck thugs headed by Jasper Swain before he was arrested and died in prison. J.T. was his nephew, the son of Swain's sister Opal. His real name is Jamie Butler, but his mother convinced him to take the Swain name instead. Maybe she thought it would put him in a better position to take over the whole family business."

"A real stage mom, huh?"

"She was a piece of work. Even her son must have thought so, since he killed her before he disappeared."

"Disappeared?"

"Law enforcement has been looking for Swain for nearly five years now. He shot Opal and disappeared into the woods. Nobody's admitted to seeing him since, although there's folks in that part of Alabama who might be inclined to see him as a folk hero." Quinn sounded disgruntled. "He's a bad guy. And he had bomb-making experience."

"Ah."

"I'll call her bosses at the network, see why she might see him as a threat to her specifically. I suppose she might have done an investigative report on his story. It's a pretty tantalizing mystery."

The sound of vehicle tires crunching up the gravel driveway drew Jim's attention. He crossed to the front window in time to see Lacey's car take the turn into the side parking area. "She's back. I'll email you the photos of her suspect list later. See if you can make anything out of them."

He turned to Katie. "Your aunt Lacey is home. Why don't you come give her a hug?"

Katie toddled over to Jim, lifting her arms to be picked up. He lifted her and pasted a smile on his face, wondering if he looked as guilty as he was starting to feel.

When he'd agreed to take this job, it had seemed a worthy cause, even if he'd have to engage in a little deception. Lacey Miles was an independent, strong-willed woman who'd just lost her sister in a bombing that the police believed had been meant for her. Her bosses had wanted to supply full-time security to her, but she'd resisted, insisting that all a security entourage would accomplish was drawing more attention to her and putting her in even more danger.

The suits at the network had disagreed. So they'd called Alexander Quinn at Campbell Cove Security, who'd apparently done some work for one of the top bosses. Quinn had made a call to Jim, who had just applied for the instructor job at the company's civilian-and-law-enforcement training academy a couple of days earlier.

"I'll admit, I wasn't sure how your experience as a child caregiver was ever going to come into play in your job," Quinn had said with a grim laugh. "But it turns out, it's the answer to a knotty problem."

Lacey Miles was in need of both security, which she refused to consider, and child care, which she was desperate to obtain. Jim Mercer was the perfect person to provide her with both.

He just had to make sure she never knew that being a nanny was only half his job.

But the problem with that was, he had to lie to her to keep her in the dark. And it was becoming harder and harder to justify those lies to himself.

Chapter Nine

Lacey felt completely drained, even though her meeting with Detective Bolling had lasted only a few minutes, as he had to be back on the road to DC for his task-force meeting that afternoon.

It hadn't been her blink-and-you'll-miss it meeting with Bolling that had left her feeling so wrung out, however. She'd made the mistake of sticking one of the DVDs he'd handed over into the backseat DVD player in Marianne's car, too impatient to wait for Katie's naptime to start looking for the blue pickup truck.

What a stupid, stupid mistake. She hadn't made it five minutes into the video before she'd felt the urge to throw up. She'd thought her own memory of the night was painfully unfiltered, but the camera's objectivity was brutal. It captured everything, all the images she'd been spared seeing that night.

"Are you okay?" Jim asked, concern warm in

his eyes when she refused his offer of a turkey sandwich for lunch.

She couldn't bear the kindness of his gaze, so she looked at Katie instead, her heart aching as she thought about what her niece had lost. At least she hadn't been there, too. At least she had a chance at the life the car bomb had stolen from her parents.

"I made the mistake of trying to watch one of the DVDs in the car," she said bluntly. "I wasn't prepared."

"I don't know how you can prepare for something like that."

She let herself look at him then, just a brief bump of gazes. "No."

"Do you think you'll want to eat later?"

She shook her head, unsure she would ever want to eat again. "I should push through these disks."

"Let me put Katie down for her nap and I'll help."

"That's not necessary."

"I'm not as close to it as you are. And I've seen worse, believe me."

She was too drained to argue. He was probably right—his objectivity would be a benefit. And if he was there watching with her, maybe she could be stronger and more objective about the videos, too.

While he coaxed Katie from her high chair, Lacey walked down the hall to the small room her brother-in-law had turned into an office. She put the set of DVDs on the desk and headed back up the hall to Katie's bedroom.

Jim had settled her in the crib and stood beside her, giving her golden curls a brush. He looked up at Lacey with a smile.

"Mind if I join you?" she asked.

"Of course not."

"Wead?" Katie asked, looking up at Jim.

"You want to read to her this time?" Jim asked Lacey.

After watching the video, she realized, the thing she needed most in the world was to cuddle Katie and remember that not everything she loved had been lost that night. Giving Jim a grateful smile, she settled in the rocking chair with Katie and picked up the book lying on the bedside table. *"Mrs. Moon's Lullaby,"* she said aloud, peering at the cover. She'd never read this one before.

"We bought it at a shop in town the other day," Jim told her. "Katie loves it."

Lacey flipped the page and started reading about Mrs. Moon telling bedtime stories to the stars. It was a charming graphic poem and Jim was right—Katie loved it. By the end, Katie was yawning her way through the final lines, then babbled softly about the pirates, snowflakes and penguins all featured in Mrs. Moon's tales until she fell asleep.

Jim had waited at the door for Lacey, his expression sympathetic. "Feeling any better?" he asked quietly as he closed the door behind her and followed her down the hall to the office.

"Yes, actually." She sat at the desk in front of the large monitor of an all-in-one computer that had belonged to Toby and motioned for Jim to pull up a nearby chair. "Now I'm just going to have to suck it up and watch these things. Were you serious about helping me?"

"Absolutely." He sat beside her. "If you want, I can grab my laptop and look through these for a blue pickup truck while you see if anything in the videos catches your attention."

"That's asking a lot of you," she said, starting to regret asking him to help. "It's not pretty."

He put his hand over hers, his palm warm and slightly rough against hers. Working hands, she thought, surprised. She hadn't expected a nanny's hands to be so calloused.

She felt a little sexist, assuming he'd be soft. If she'd learned anything from the time she'd spent caring for Katie since her parents' deaths, it was that child care was hard. It was rewarding but difficult. And to choose to do the job as a vocation surely required strength, stamina and a willingness to get your hands dirty.

In no hurry to get to the videos again, she let her gaze slide up his body. The Marine Corps training still showed, from his sinewy, muscular arms to the sharp gaze that met hers when her roving eyes finally reached his face.

He was still holding her hand, she realized, in no hurry to let go.

"You don't have to do this today." His voice was gentle, and his fingers flexed over hers. "Take a day. Get it out of your head and start fresh."

She started to move her hand out from under his, but somehow, she ended up turning her palm upward to grip his hand. "I need to get this over with. Putting it off won't make it any easier. It might just make it worse."

He ran his thumb lightly across the inside of her wrist. It was a gentle, almost thoughtless caress, but the touch detonated a string of tiny explosions along her nervous system.

She was attracted to him. It was wrong on so many levels, and nothing she could ever let herself think of pursuing, but she couldn't deny it anymore.

He was handsome. He was strong and kind. And he smelled delicious, a heady blend of crisp soap and pure, masculine musk.

He was watching her with a gaze that surely missed nothing, including her helpless attraction to him, but he didn't move closer, didn't press the advantage. Even though he could have. Even though she'd have probably rewarded the daring with a helpless response of her own.

She made herself pull away, squaring her shoulders against her own weakness. "Katie won't sleep that long. Let's get as much done as we can."

"Okay. Let me grab my laptop."

The room seemed bigger and colder when he left, an uncomfortable reminder of how large a presence he was becoming in her life.

It was the last thing she'd planned for, nothing she'd hoped for. It was a complication in a life already burdened by a heavy load of complexity.

What the hell was she supposed to do with these unexpected feelings about Jim Mercer?"

He came back into the room, filling the space he'd left before. Overfilling it, consuming all the air until Lacey felt as if she couldn't draw a full breath. "Where do you want to start?"

Struggling against the undertow of attraction, she pulled out a disk and put it in the computer's DVD drive. "I've watched the first thirty minutes of this one. I think it's probably a good idea to get to the part after the traffic starts slowing down for people to rubberneck the crime scene. That's when I remember the truck showing up."

For the next hour, Lacey steeled herself against the images and sounds of the police video of her sister's scene of death, trying hard not to give in and watch through her fingers as if she were a frightened child. But it was wrenching and difficult, every bit as difficult as it had been when she'd first stuck the DVD into the SUV's backseat player.

"There you are," Jim murmured.

Lacey paused the video she'd been watching and rolled the desk chair closer to where he sat. Sure enough, she spotted her own dark red trench coat on the left side of the video frame. She was pacing near the crime-scene tape, her cell phone to her ear. When her relentless pacing turned her video self to face the camera, Lacey saw a pale oval looking back at her, shock and strain lining her features.

Sympathy rolled off Jim in waves, swamping her. She couldn't allow herself to meet his eyes or she'd be lost.

"Look for a limousine," she murmured, keeping her gaze glued to the laptop screen. "The pickup truck comes shortly after that."

This was a different angle from the one in her dream, she realized as she spotted the limousine she'd dreamed about come into view. "That's it," she said."

Jim paused the video. "Can you make out the license-plate number?"

She peered at the screen, but she couldn't make out the number. "It's not a governmental plate," she said aloud. "I thought it would be."

"Is that a *W*?" He pointed to the blurry first letter of the plate. "And those could be two *T*s together, couldn't they?"

Sudden excitement fluttered in her chest. Could the limousine belong to one of the Whittier brothers? They were both spending a lot of time in the capital these days, building their networks as they ran for two open seats in western Connecticut.

"Does that say Whittier?" Jim asked.

Something about his tone struck her as odd, but she was too excited by the prospect of a lead to give it any further thought. She'd gotten so focused on the blue pickup truck that the possibility of a different clue hadn't even crossed her mind.

If the limousine belonged to one of the Whittier brothers, it might mean that she was on the right track. Even though nobody, not even the most vehement of the Whittiers' detractors, had suggested either of the brothers or their family might be involved in anything as criminal as murder, Lacey hadn't been able to shake the feeling that the family's ruthless pursuit of public office—and the power that came with it—might have no upper limits. The brothers might be all charisma and smiles, but their father and uncles hadn't made their fortunes following all the rules. Attaining the sort of wealth and position the Whittier family had amassed over the past half century hadn't happened without some brutal methods.

Were the brothers or their political handlers just as willing to get blood on their hands?

"You were right," Jim said, his voice breaking into her thoughts. She saw he'd let the video run a few moments longer and had paused it on the image of a blue pickup truck. "There's the truck."

She leaned closer. "It's the same truck I saw the day I went to Frederick," she said after closer study. "See the dent on the front panel on the driver's side? I didn't remember that, exactly, but I think that's why I've felt so certain it was the same truck each time."

"It's a Toyota Tacoma. Looks as if it's had a bit of wear and tear, so I'd say it's probably a few years old."

"I'll call Detective Bolling." Lacey reached for the phone.

As she dialed Bolling's number, Jim ran the

video ahead a few frames, leaning toward the screen to peer at the images. "I can't make out any numbers on the license plate. It looks as if there's mud splattered across the plate, obscuring the numbers."

"Intentional?" she asked as she waited for Bolling to answer.

"Hard to say."

"Bolling," came the detective's voice in her ear.

"Detective Bolling, it's Lacey Miles." She told him what she'd found and included the time stamps on the video. "Was anyone recording license-plate numbers at the scene?"

"Not specifically, but I can have the original video enhanced at the times you mentioned to see if we can clear anything up." Bolling's voice dipped a half octave with sympathy. "I know watching that footage can't be easy for you."

"It's not," she admitted. "But I think it's worth doing in the long run."

"Don't push yourself too far," Bolling warned. "Remember, we have a whole task force of people looking into the bombing."

"What about the Whittiers? Have you had any dealings with them?"

Bolling was silent for a long moment. "Obviously, even if I were looking into any allegations about any of the Whittier family, I couldn't discuss it with anyone outside the investigation without departmental sanction."

Which meant they were suspicious that the Whittiers might be involved in something at the very least shady, but they were under strong pressure to keep it under wraps—and maybe even sit on the investigation completely.

"I understand," she said. "Thanks for listening. You'll let me know if you find out anything about the blue truck?"

"We'll check it out and I'll get back to you one way or the other." Bolling sounded relieved that Lacey didn't seem inclined to push him further on the question of the Whittier brothers.

He clearly didn't know her very well.

After she hung up, she turned to look at Jim. "I think the DC police may be suspicious of the Whittier brothers."

"What do you think they're involved with?"

"Insider trading at the very least, although I wasn't able to come up with proof of it. But their stock-market investments seemed to have thrived while other people were losing their life savings during the stock-market crash several years ago. It's as if everything they touch turns to gold."

"Well, that eventually came back to haunt old King Midas, didn't it?"

"It did," she said with a smile. The expression

felt strange on her face, as if her skin was about to crack from the unfamiliar strain.

He moved closer to her, one hand lifting hesitantly to her face. When she didn't pull away, he brought his other hand up to cradle her jaw between his palms. "Tell me what you want to do now."

She stared up at him, surprised by the question itself, and the intensity of his gaze as he asked it. Nobody had asked her that question since Marianne and Toby had died, she realized. Not her employers, not Marianne and Toby's attorney, not the social worker who'd helped her get custody of Katie, not even her sister's friends who'd shown up for the funeral. They'd told her what was going to happen, how things should go, what she should do and what she shouldn't.

But nobody had once asked her what it was that she wanted to do.

"I want to find out who did this heinous thing," she answered bluntly. "I want to make them pay. I want them in jail or dead and posing no more danger to me or Katie. That's what I want."

His lips curved in a whisper of a smile. "Then let's make that happen."

For a long moment, he gazed down at her, his expression a promise she wanted to grasp with both hands and hold on to for dear life. She hadn't realized how much she'd needed someone to listen to her, to believe she could find justice for Marianne and Toby, instead of telling her to keep her head down and let the professionals do the job for her.

She was a professional, damn it. She might not be trained in law-enforcement procedures, but she knew about ferreting out hidden truths in desperately dangerous places. She had an advantage the police didn't. *She* was the intended victim, and she knew herself and her history better than anyone else in the world.

His gaze shifted, drifting down to her lips. Heat flooded her body, head to toe, as she let her own gaze dip to his mouth. She imagined his lips moving over hers, teasing her with whisper-soft kisses, coaxing a response she knew she wouldn't be able to resist.

She waited for him to realize just what sort of tense heat was building between them. Surely he would move away, murmur some soft excuse or maybe make a little joke to snap the tension.

But he moved closer instead, his breath hot on her lips. She told herself to be the one to back away, to act with good sense, to make the tension-breaking joke.

Instead, she stepped closer, closing the heated space between them, lifting to her toes as he threaded his fingers through the hair at the back of her head and tugged her into his arms.

He brushed his lips against hers, the faintest of caresses that left her aching for more. He teased her with another soft kiss, a little nip at her bottom lip with his mouth that promised amazing things.

She curled her fingers into the hard steel of his shoulder muscles and pulled him closer, needing to feel the slide of his body against hers. He wrapped one long arm around her waist, guiding her closer as he took her mouth in a long, thorough kiss.

She was drowning in him, in his kiss, in the way his hard body moved with sensual intent against hers. She felt something press hard into her buttocks and realized he'd edged her back against the desk.

The desk where her dead brother-in-law's computer held a disk detailing his gruesome death, along with her sister's.

Cold rushed in, as if someone had opened a floodgate to let in a torrent of icy water. She stiffened against Jim's body, and he let her go, taking a step back from her.

She gazed at him, pushing one shaky hand through her hair. She tried to think of something to say, maybe that awkward joke she'd been planning before they'd acted on the fierce heat roiling between them.

But she could come up with nothing.

"Not the right time, huh?" Jim managed a smile that looked as uncertain as she felt.

"No."

"I should check on Katie. She should be waking up from her nap soon."

Lacey nodded, afraid to move for fear her wobbly knees would betray her. "Okay. I'll take these disks up to my office and finish watching there, so Katie doesn't see or hear anything…" She let her words trail off, pain throbbing in her throat.

"Okay." Jim started to leave, but he stopped and turned back to face her. "I should probably apologize for what just happened and promise never to let it happen again. But I'm not sure I'd mean it."

She didn't know what to say in response. She could hardly disagree, because she didn't feel very sorry about it herself. Nor could she promise she'd never give in to her desires again.

His lips curving slightly at the corners, he left the room, taking all the air with him.

Lacey gripped the edge of the desk until her trembling limbs could hold her, then she grabbed the disks, including the one in the computer, and headed upstairs to the locked room on the second floor.

She wasn't sure which images were going to haunt her more, the merciless videos of the aftermath of the car bomb or the gentle, tender way Jim had soothed away some of the pain with his tempting kisses.

She stopped at the locked door, looking down at the disks she held in her hand. She'd seen terrible things in her life, in her career as a reporter. Aftermaths of deaths just as brutal as the ones that had claimed her sister and brother-in-law.

She could handle this. For Katie's sake, for Marianne's and Toby's, she *would* handle it. The truth about what had really happened that night, and at whose hands it had come to pass, might be there in those videos, waiting for the right person to see the right thing and make the right connection.

She would be that person. She had to.

Jim had told her she could do it. He'd made her believe it.

Pulling her key from her pocket, she inserted it into the dead-bolt lock and gave it a turn. It seemed to stick for a second before the lock disengaged. She then inserted a thin piece of metal into the small hole in the doorknob to disengage the knob's lock, feeling a little silly as she did so. If the dead bolt wasn't enough to keep someone from getting into the room, the doorknob lock certainly wouldn't.

Closing the door behind her, she stood still a moment in front of the doorway, taking in the whiteboard and the words printed across its surface.

Nothing seemed out of place, but she had a strange feeling that something in the room was different.

She walked slowly to the desk, where her laptop sat closed on its dented, well-worn surface. Setting the DVDs next to the computer, she lifted the lid of the laptop and looked at the screen. It was the same lock screen as usual. Nothing different.

Except...

It was a faint scent she could smell over the general mustiness of the room, she realized. Crisp soap. Heady musk. Clean and masculine.

It smelled like Jim.

Chapter Ten

Katie was restless and fussy after her nap, refusing the peanut-butter crackers Jim offered her and throwing her sliced carrot pieces onto the floor with her cup of milk. He gave up on trying to coax her to eat, recognizing her mood for what it was—a child's uncanny ability to sense tension in the adults around her.

Instead, he took her back into the parlor and sat in the old rocking chair with her on his lap, humming an old Marine Corps marching cadence under his breath until she'd stopped fussing and settled down for a cuddle.

He had worse luck trying to calm his own restless nerves. What the hell had he been thinking, kissing Lacey that way? He had been behaving like a teenage boy who didn't have a clue how to control his raging hormones. She was his boss, for Pete's sake!

And he was supposed to be protecting her and

Katie, not trying to charm his way into Lacey's bed. He was damn fortunate she hadn't fired him on the spot.

She wanted you, too, a rebellious voice whispered in his ear.

Maybe so, but she, at least, had been wise enough to get her desires under control and put a stop to what was happening.

Between his growing guilt about his own lies of omission, Lacey's ongoing grief and anxiety, and whatever emotions and desires had fueled their make-out session in the office a little while earlier, there were a whole lot of conflicted vibes for poor Katie to pick up on these days. Maybe he should try to get her out of the house for a while. They could play in the park in Cherry Grove for an hour or so, then maybe grab takeout at the diner to bring home for dinner.

Lacey came down the stairs, pausing at the landing to look at him cuddling Katie, one golden eyebrow lifted. "I thought she just got up from her nap?"

"We're just de-stressing," he said lightly. "In fact, I was thinking I could take her into town, to the park. There are some swings there, and places for her to run and play. What do you say? I could grab us something to eat for dinner when we're done."

The look of relief on Lacey's face made his gut clench. Clearly, she was happy to get rid of him for a while. Was she working up to firing him altogether?

"That's a good idea. I need to do a little research, and I can probably get more done by myself. Be sure to bundle her up—it's cold out there."

"Will do," he said with a smile that made his face feel as if it were about to crack.

The day had warmed enough for the remaining patches of snow to melt, but the higher temperatures would be long gone by dark. If the local weather forecasters were right, they'd see more snow before the end of the week. Jim liked a good snowball fight as much as the next kid from western North Carolina, but snowfall made his job protecting Lacey and Katie a little harder, especially if it managed to knock out the power.

He took the opportunity to call Alexander Quinn from the car, catching him up on what he'd learned while watching the crime-scene video with Lacey, leaving out the part about the kiss, of course.

"The insider-trading allegations are probably true," Quinn said bluntly. "But I'm guessing there's no way to prove it, and the Whittiers know it."

"So you don't think they're likely suspects."

"Well, they're not obvious suspects. Let's put it that way."

"Most of the tabloid trash about them may or may not be true, but surely none of it is enough to inspire murder."

"No, but I've just gotten my hands on a raw copy of footage from a report Lacey Miles was working on a couple of months ago."

"Was working on?"

"My sources say that the Whittiers sicced their lawyers on the network and the report got nixed."

"With no respect to whether the report was true or not?"

"Apparently the Whittiers weren't the only people applying pressure. I'll upload the video to the company cloud storage and email you the link. It'll give you a better idea why Ms. Miles considers the Whittiers as possible suspects."

Jim glanced in the rearview mirror. Katie was quiet in her car seat, her gaze directed out the window. Jim was using his Bluetooth headset to keep her from hearing Quinn's side of the conversation, but she'd proved sensitive to tension, and right now, Jim's car was chock-full of volatile emotions.

"Any chatter from al Adar around the time of the bombing?" he asked Quinn.

"No, but al Adar has learned from the mistakes of their terrorist predecessors. There was very little communication between known cells at all around the time of the bombing. Which may mean everything or nothing. We just don't know yet."

Jim thought about the third suspect he'd seen on Lacey's whiteboard. "And what about J.T. Swain?"

"I've arranged a meeting between you and a couple of people who should be able to answer a lot of your questions about Swain. They're going to be up in Washington on business later in the week. I'll text you their number so you can set up the meeting. Their names are Ben and Isabel Scanlon. Ben knew J.T. Swain when they were boys, and he also spent almost a year undercover among the Swain clan, trying to bring down their criminal enterprise from the inside."

"And lived to tell?"

"Well, he had some help from his partner in the FBI. Who happens to be his wife now."

"Okay. I'll give them a call."

"You sound…strange."

Jim grimaced. Of course a man like Quinn would pick up on even the tiniest hint of turmoil in his voice. "It's just proving hard to keep secrets, you know?"

"You mean your real reason for taking the nanny job."

"Yeah."

"Is she suspicious?"

"I don't think so." He thought about the way Lacey had been behaving when she came back downstairs from the locked room. He had assumed her slight reserve had been about the kiss they'd shared earlier, but what if he was wrong? What if she'd somehow figured out that he'd been in her room earlier that morning?

He'd taken care to leave everything as he'd found it, and he was pretty sure she wouldn't have been able to find a single piece of paper out of place. But even the most seasoned of operatives could make a mistake, and Jim was pretty new to the job.

Had she found something in the room that had given away his earlier presence? Was that why she was so eager to get him out of the house?

"Jim?"

"I'm here," he said quickly. "I'm nearly at the park, so I'll have to talk to you later."

"Okay. Keep me apprised of everything you find out." Quinn's words sounded a lot like a warning.

"Will do." Jim hung up the phone and parked in one of the slots at the edge of the green park, just a few yards away from the swings. He eased

Katie from her car seat and held her hand as they walked down the gravel walkway to the swings.

"Wings!" Katie exclaimed, raising a joyous face to Jim. "Wings?"

"Yes, ma'am. We're going to play on the swings."

Katie tugged her hand away as they reached the swings, stopping in front of the one swing on the set that was made for toddlers, complete with a high-backed bucket seat. She lifted her arms to him and he put her in the seat and gave it a push.

"Wing!" Katie exclaimed, wriggling insistently. He took it as a plea to let her swing higher.

He gave her a little sturdier push, and the swing flew a little higher, making Katie laugh with delight.

Jim tried to relax, tried to push away the cares of his world and just enjoy this sweet, magic moment when he'd made a little girl laugh with simple joy.

He would find a way to protect Katie and her mercurial, fascinating aunt. Whatever it took.

SHE HAD CHASED violent warlords up the mountains of Kaziristan to obtain an interview. She had braved the icy disdain of the Connecticut neighbors while trying to gain access to Justin and Carson Whittier in hopes of getting their side of the scandalous rumors swirling around their family. She'd faced down the barely leashed violence of the ragtag remains of what had once been a brutal family of drug dealers and gunrunners.

So why was it so hard to open the door to the room she'd given Jim to use and find out what he was hiding?

She tried his door handle. It gave easily, the door creaking partially open. Lacey pressed her forehead against the door frame, debating her next move. His door wasn't locked. He wasn't trying to keep anyone out.

Surely that meant he didn't have anything to hide.

Just go in there and take a look around. You're an investigative reporter. Investigate.

She gave the door a push. It swung all the way inward, bumping lightly against the doorstop attached to the baseboard of the bedroom wall.

Inside, she found a neatly made bed—military neat, she thought. No clutter on the bedside table, just a small alarm clock next to the lamp.

She opened the top drawer of the nightstand. Drugstore-brand lip balm. A nearly full pack of breath mints. A slightly dog-eared paperback novel with a cover and title that screamed action thriller.

Nothing unexpected. Until she opened the

next drawer down. Inside was a large black box that nearly filled the whole drawer. She didn't need to open it to know what it was.

A handgun case.

It was locked, of course. A former Marine wouldn't leave his firearm unsecured.

She didn't find any ammunition in the nightstand drawers. But she came across several boxes of .40-caliber rounds in the middle drawer of the dresser at the foot of his bed.

Sinking onto the edge of the bed, she stared at the boxes of ammo and tried to think clearly. He was a former Marine, so of course he'd probably have a personal weapon. Probably had a concealed-carry license, as well.

But he was here as a nanny, not as a Marine. What was he thinking, bringing a weapon into her home without letting her know? It was easily grounds for dismissal, and she doubted he'd bother to argue.

And then what? She'd have to find another nanny. She'd lose days, maybe weeks, of investigation trying to settle her domestic affairs.

Maybe he had a good explanation. Maybe she should wait until he got home to hear what he had to say.

Maybe she didn't want to believe the man who'd kissed her with such sweet passion just a couple of hours ago could be playing on her emotions for his own purposes.

She heard the sound of a car door closing outside, followed by Katie's happy, excited chattering. Her first instinct was to jump up and leave Jim's room to avoid being caught snooping, but she made herself sit still. She left the dresser drawer open, revealing the spoils of her investigation.

"Lacey?" Jim's voice carried from the front parlor.

"In here," she answered, waiting for him to reach her.

He stopped in the open doorway, his hand still curled around Katie's. His gaze moved to the open dresser drawer, then flicked back to meet hers.

What she saw there made her heart sink. He didn't look offended or outraged by her snooping.

He looked guilty as hell.

She leaned forward, pushing his dresser drawer shut, and pasted on a bright smile for her niece. "Did you have fun at the park, sweet pea?"

"Wings!" Katie responded with a look of rapturous delight lighting up her face.

"She likes to swing," Jim said.

"Yes. I know." Lacey picked up her niece and

edged past Jim into the hallway. "Let's get you out of this coat, baby."

Safely alone with Katie in the nursery, she locked the bedroom door behind her and helped the little girl out of the thick jacket and pants in which Jim had dressed her for their trip to the park, concentrating on keeping her mind free of any thoughts about Jim Mercer or what she planned to do next.

Katie was the priority. She had to be. Lacey was all the family her niece had left in the world, and she took that reality seriously. Which meant that she couldn't take chances with her own safety or Katie's.

Was Jim a threat to their safety? If she'd seen anything but guilt on his face, she might believe otherwise.

A few minutes later, there was a light knock on the door. "Lacey?"

She pressed her lips into a thin line, her treacherous mind going directly to those electric moments a few hours earlier when Jim had kissed her in Toby's office. And she'd let him, without putting up any sort of resistance.

"Not now," she said.

"You're just going to spend the rest of the night in there with Katie?" he asked. "She hasn't had dinner yet. Or a bath."

"Go the hell away, Jim."

Katie looked up at her, a look of confusion on her sweet face. Lacey picked her up, cuddling her close.

"It's okay, baby," she soothed, carrying Katie to the rocking chair next to the crib. "Everything is going to be okay."

As Katie settled down, Lacey forced her scattered thoughts into some semblance of order. Should she call the police? On what grounds? Because a former Marine who probably had all his paperwork in perfect order had brought a firearm into her house without telling her?

She wasn't some wilting flower who couldn't deal with robust self-defense. She knew how to handle a weapon herself, though she had decided not to carry a weapon of her own. She had no problem with law-abiding citizens exercising their second-amendment rights.

But Jim had kept something from her. More than just the presence of a pistol in her home, if the look of regret and guilt in his expression was anything to go by.

Just what was it that he was really hiding?

"Jim?" Katie queried softly a few moments later.

"We'll go see Jim in just a minute," Lacey promised, meaning it. If she really wanted to know what Jim was hiding, she wasn't going to find out by hiding in Katie's room.

She gave her niece a quick diaper change, soothing the worried look on the little girl's face with a few kisses and a quick raspberry blown against her belly, which made Katie giggle madly.

Jim was in the kitchen when she and Katie entered, standing at the sink looking out the window at the backyard, where the last pitiful remains of Marvin the Snowman was giving up the ghost.

He turned at the sound of Lacey's footsteps. "I'm sorry."

"Katie might be ready for that snack now," Lacey suggested, setting the girl down on the floor.

Katie toddled over to Jim and held her arms up. He glanced at Lacey, as if asking for permission.

Lacey gave a slight nod, her heart aching at the pure delighted affection she saw in her niece's face when Jim swung her up in his arms.

"Want to try those peanut-butter crackers again, Katiebug?"

"Mmm," Katie said with a grin.

Jim put her in the high chair and went to the cabinet to retrieve the box of crackers and the jar of peanut butter.

Lacey crossed to his side. "Why did you take this job?"

He paused in the middle of opening the jar of peanut butter. "Because I was hired to do so."

Lacey glanced at Katie and lowered her voice. "By whom?"

"By a company called Campbell Cove Security. I was already being interviewed for a position as an instructor at the company's civilian-and-law-enforcement academy when the company received a request for a security expert who could double as a nanny."

"So they sent you?"

He nodded and finished opening the jar of peanut butter. He took a butter knife and started to spread the peanut butter over the first of a small stack of crackers.

"Do you even have experience as a nanny?"

"That part of my background is entirely true," he answered quietly. "After my father's unexpected death, I raised my younger siblings while my mother worked. After I left the Marine Corps, after college, I really did work as a child caregiver for a Kentucky couple before I was contacted by Campbell Cove Security."

"Who hired Campbell Cove Security to protect me?"

He glanced at her but didn't answer.

"I know nothing about that security company," she pressed on. "I very much doubt your boss there would send you as a double agent on his or her own initiative. So who hired you?"

Jim put together the last of the peanut-butter crackers and released a faint sigh. "Your network."

Of course. She'd said no to their offer of security, so her bosses had taken it upon themselves to give her security anyway.

"I don't think they should have been deceptive about it," he added.

"That's rich, coming from you."

He looked as if he wanted to argue, but he kept his cool, turning to face her. He lowered his voice to a near whisper, his gaze slanting toward Katie. "You're in danger. So is Katie. I can help you both."

She lowered her voice, as well. "So, after your deceptive manner of getting inside my house, I'm supposed to continue paying you to take care of my niece and allow you to moonlight as our bodyguard? Is that what you're suggesting?"

He gave her a level look. "Pretty much, yeah."

Clamping her mouth shut, she turned away from him and grabbed a clean sippy cup from the cabinet nearby. She filled it with milk from the refrigerator and turned back to face Jim. "I'm not stupid, you know. I didn't make the choice to refuse security lightly. I'm trying to keep a low profile here in Cherry Grove. If I were suddenly followed around town by an entourage of armed men, that would draw far more attention to me and my niece than I want."

"And those security guards might impede your investigation into your sister's murder."

She met his gaze. "You *did* pick the lock on my situation room."

His lips curved slightly at the corners before he brought his expression back under control. "You didn't make it nearly as easy to figure out what you were up to as I did. All you had to do was open my door and snoop around my bedroom, while I had to pull out the lock-pick tools to get to your secrets."

"A locked door is an invitation to enter and look around?"

"So, apparently, is an unlocked one."

It was her turn to fight the urge to smile. Damn him.

"I'm going to let you continue your job here," she said quietly as she fit the lid on the sippy cup. "Both of them. I'm even willing to consider allowing you to assist me in my investigation, on the condition that you don't tell your boss or my boss anything else about the investigation."

"My boss has access to information that might help us."

"I gave you my condition."

He didn't look happy, but he nodded. "Okay."

She handed the crackers and the cup of milk to Katie, who began consuming both with crumb-flinging eagerness. Turning back to Jim, she leveled her gaze with his. "There's one more thing."

His brow furrowed. "What?"

"If you think I'm ever going to trust you again on a personal level, you can forget it. From now on, there's nothing but business between us."

Chapter Eleven

"So, you know by now that I'm concentrating on three possible assailants," Lacey said the next morning as they sat side by side—but carefully not touching—on the steps of the farmhouse's back porch while they watched Katie run around chasing squirrels that had ventured out that chilly morning to pick up walnuts that had fallen from the two large trees growing in the backyard.

"Yup. The Whittiers, al Adar and J.T. Swain."

"I assume by now you've familiarized yourself with all three?" The dry tone of her voice made him writhe inwardly. She would not be quick to forgive him for his lies of omission. If she ever did.

No matter. He deserved her mistrust.

"I was already familiar with al Adar. I've caught up, mostly, on the other two."

"There may be a few things you don't know about the Whittier brothers."

"Maybe not." He'd risked using the house internet connection to watch the video Alexander Quinn had uploaded to Campbell Cove Security's cloud storage. A far less careworn Lacey Miles had delved into the details of a Whittier Enterprises real-estate-development deal that was supposed to benefit hundreds of lower-to-middle-class residents of the Bronx. "I know you suspect the Whittiers' real-estate-development company changed the plans for a housing development near the Bronx in order to facilitate the cover-up of a mysterious death."

Lacey stared at him. "How the hell could you know that?"

"Because I saw the raw footage of the report you had planned to do."

Lacey looked away, turning her cool profile to him. Silence extended between them until he was ready to speak just to break the tension. But she spoke first. "Your company was able to get their hands on that footage? It must be better connected than I realized."

"I think maybe you're right."

Katie lost interest in chasing the elusive squirrels and came running over to the porch, launching herself into Jim's arms. He settled her on his knees, where she beamed at Lacey. "Snowman," she said firmly.

"I'm afraid Marvin's almost melted away," Lacey said with an exaggerated frown.

"Make snowman!" Katie insisted. "Mahbin."

Lacey glanced at Jim. He shot her a sympathetic look and shrugged one shoulder.

"Make Mahbin!" Katie demanded.

"We'll have to wait for it to snow again, sweetie." Lacey reached over to zip up Katie's jacket just as Jim moved his hands to do the same thing, and her fingers brushed his, setting off sparks. He wasn't sure if the sensation was the real result of static or just his body's electric reaction to her touch.

He wasn't sure it mattered.

Lacey dropped her hand quickly, flicking a swift glance Jim's way before she settled her gaze on Katie. "I bet you're hungry, aren't you, baby?"

Distracted by the demands of her stomach, Katie nodded.

"I'll get her settled in her high chair if you'll heat up some chicken-noodle soup for her," Lacey said, reaching out to take Katie from his arms.

Katie didn't fuss when Lacey took her inside, though she did shoot Jim a questioning look, as if she didn't understand why he wasn't the one carrying her through the mudroom door.

While Lacey helped Katie shed her snowsuit, Jim heated leftover chicken-noodle soup and poured it into one of Katie's favorite bowls. He set it in front of her and took a step back, pretending to watch Katie dig into the soup while he secretly took every chance he could get to look at Lacey.

To say she was still angry with him was an understatement. But at least they were talking. It was a start.

"How much of the footage was your company able to get their hands on?" Lacey asked a few minutes later when she joined him near the refrigerator. She pulled apple juice from the refrigerator and poured a cup for Katie.

"I think maybe all of it."

She slanted a quick look at him before she handed Katie the drink and sat in the chair to her right.

Jim took a seat across from Lacey. "I can show you."

She shook her head. "I've seen it, remember. I'm the one who put it together."

"Why didn't the network let you air it?"

"Because the Whittiers threatened to take the whole network down if we did. It went all the way up to the network suits, who capitulated."

"I thought the press was supposed to be the ones who spoke truth to power and all that."

"I can't prove this, but I think someone in the Whittier clan applied a little leverage to someone pretty damned high up in the network."

Jim frowned. "You mean blackmail?"

"That's exactly what I mean." Lacey grabbed a paper towel from the roll hanging on the wall and crossed to Katie to mop up the soupy mess the little girl was making. "I can't think of any other reason the network would have put a stop to my report."

"Any idea who? Or what?"

She shook her head. "I may be an investigative reporter, but I learned a long time ago that indulging in behind-the-scenes gossip is a great way to lose your job. I've always steered clear of that sort of thing, and all my coworkers know it. They don't even bother to whisper anything anymore."

"But it's a case now, isn't it? You could approach it as if it's something you're investigating, not gossip."

"I have to work with those people. I can't start digging around in their personal lives and pasts just because I'm sort of suspicious about why my investigation was shut down. If they're being blackmailed, it's probably about something in their lives I don't want or need to know about.

I'll find another way to get to the truth about the Whittiers. Whatever it is. And when I do, not even the network is going to be able to stop me from revealing it."

Which explained why the Whittiers might want to put her out of action for good, Jim thought. "Okay. So let's change gears. J.T. Swain. What if I told you I could get you a meeting with someone who probably knows more about Swain and his history than anyone else in the world?"

She gave him a skeptical look. "The person who knows the most about Swain is a former FBI agent who knew him as a kid and also went undercover with Swain's organization for a while. Ben Scanlon. But, believe me, I tried to talk to Scanlon and his wife, who's the next best expert on Swain, when I was doing my investigation into his disappearance. Neither of them would talk to me."

"They'll talk to you now. I already have a meeting set up."

She stared at him, disbelieving. "I spent months trying to get an interview with them. How did you manage it?"

"My boss at Campbell Cove Security has a knack for making the impossible happen."

"When will they meet me? And where?"

"Us," Jim corrected. "They'll meet us."

The scowl that creased Lacey's forehead was impressive, but Jim waited for her to figure out the reality: if she wanted to talk to the Scanlons, she was going to have to accept Jim as a partner in the investigation.

Her lips finally pressed into a thin line. "Fine. When and where?"

"They're going to be in the area later this week. I'm supposed to call and set it up."

"The sooner, the better," she said firmly.

"Yeah, I figured that."

Now finished with her soup, Katie had turned the bowl upside down and was using her spoon to bang on the bottom of the bowl. Jim gently extricated her makeshift drum from her hands, earning a scowl nearly as intimidating as her aunt's.

"I'll call as soon as I get Katiebug cleaned up and settled for her nap."

Lacey stood. "Go make the call. I'll take care of Katie."

"You sure?"

She nodded. "Go. The sooner the better, remember."

Jim deposited the bowl in the sink for a rinse, then pulled out his cell phone and retreated to the front parlor to make his call. He reached Ben Scanlon on the first ring.

"I've been expecting your call." Scanlon's

voice was deep, his words edged with a twang that reminded Jim of a gunnery sergeant he'd known in the Marine Corps, a Texan through and through. "Isabel and I will be in Washington for a seminar on domestic terrorism this weekend, but we thought we'd drive rather than fly. Make a road trip out of it. We'll be overnighting in Strasburg on Wednesday. I've been taking a look at the map—we could take a detour on our way into DC and meet up with you in Leesburg Thursday around noon."

"Leesburg on Thursday at noon. We'll be there."

There was a brief pause. "Who's we?"

"I want to bring Lacey Miles with me."

"She's a reporter." Scanlon said the word as if it was a pejorative.

"She's a woman whose sister was murdered in her place," Jim said with more heat than he'd intended. "Her life is still in danger, and she wants to know if there's any way J.T. Swain could be behind it."

"I can tell you now, I don't think he is."

"I think Lacey will want to get all the facts and make that decision for herself." Jim looked up to find Lacey standing in the doorway to the parlor, her clothes a little rumpled and her hair flying wildly. Katie wasn't with her, so she must have been successful putting her niece down for a nap.

She gazed back at him, questions flickering in her cool gray eyes.

"Okay. Thursday at noon in Leesburg. I'll text you the place when we pick it out." Scanlon's voice deepened a notch. "I'm not looking to end up on the network news here, Mercer. The Swain family may not be running Halloran County anymore, but there are enough of them left to make life dangerous for us. We're trying to stay off their radar as much as we can."

"Understood. This isn't about a news story."

"Good. I'll text you soon."

Jim hung up and looked at Lacey, who'd moved to the armchair across from where he sat. "Thursday in Leesburg at noon."

She gave a brief nod. "We'll have to take Katie along."

"Of course."

There was a brief softening of her eyes before her cool reserve returned. He quelled his disappointment. He'd earned her distrust, and if he wanted the tension between them to ease again, he'd have to be patient. He knew with time he could prove to her that he was serious about keeping her and Katie safe.

But there was no chance in hell she'd ever risk letting him get close to her again. And now that the reality of that fact began to sink in, Jim was starting to realize just how much he wanted to find out how far their mutual attraction could take them.

LEESBURG ANIMAL PARK was a surprising choice of venue for a meeting, but by the time Katie had petted goats and lambs and worn herself out playing with other toddlers in the play area, she fell asleep in Jim's arms halfway through her picnic lunch, leaving Lacey, Jim and the Scanlons to talk in peace.

"I wish we could've brought Delia with us," Isabel Scanlon commented, her tea-brown eyes softening as she looked at Katie sleeping in Jim's lap. "She just turned three last fall. But the seminar is all work, and she'll be a lot happier home with her cousins."

"I appreciate your agreeing to talk to me." Lacey pushed aside the half-eaten remains of her lunch and met Ben Scanlon's gaze. His smoky-blue eyes were sharp but kind, and she felt the last of her tension seeping away. "I'm not going to use anything you tell me in a news report. This is purely for me. I need to know if J.T. Swain could have been involved in the bombing that killed my sister. In revenge for my report that dredged up his story. I know public reaction to my report put Swain back onto the active investigations list for several law-enforcement agencies. Would he want revenge for that? Enough to try to kill me?"

Ben and Isabel Scanlon looked at each other. In that brief meeting of gazes, they seemed to hold an entire conversation before Ben said, "He's capable of setting a car bomb. But I've spent the past few years watching for any sign that he's back in business, and I've come across nothing. I think he's holed up somewhere in the mountains, living off the land and bothering nobody."

"You think he's retired." Jim sounded skeptical.

"He killed his mother because she turned him into a monster," Ben said quietly, sadness tinting his voice. "When we were kids, we were best friends. Jamie was a good kid from a bad family. But his mother thought he was growing up soft. She blamed his father, who was an outsider, for turning her son into a normal human being."

As Ben's voice faltered, Isabel reached out and covered his hand with hers. He seemed to draw strength from her touch, his shoulders squaring and his chin lifting.

"J.T. Swain's real name is Jamie Butler. He didn't take the name Swain until he was older. His mother, Opal, had nothing but contempt for her husband, so she had Jamie's name legally changed to her own maiden name."

"She wanted her son to be part of the family business?" Jim guessed.

"So much so that, when Jamie and I were eight years old, Opal took him out in her truck, gave him a loaded gun and goaded him into shooting the sheriff of Halloran County. To prove he was a true Swain."

Lacey frowned. "You mean Bennett Allen was killed by a child?"

"Yes. I saw it happen."

"But…" Lacey felt ill as realization dawned. In her research into J.T. Swain and the Swain family, the story of Bennett Allen's murder had been a showcase of just how depraved the Swain family could be. Allen had been murdered in the driveway of his own home, in front of his young son. "You're Bennett Allen's son?"

"Yes. After my father's death, my mother remarried, and my stepfather adopted me. Changed my last name. There were times over the years when I almost believed my father's murder had been nothing but a bad dream. That my mother and stepfather had moved us all to Texas for job opportunities, not so that the Swains couldn't find me and make sure I never remembered what I saw that night."

"How did you end up undercover among the

Swains?" Jim asked. He was lightly stroking Katie's hair. She looked so right in Jim's arms, as if being there was the most natural thing on earth for her. Lacey felt a hard ache forming in the center of her chest as she contemplated how difficult it would be to separate her niece from Jim when the time came for him to move on to a different job.

Hadn't he thought about the consequences of his lies? Hadn't he realized that Katie might grow so attached to him that he would hurt her by walking away?

Jim's gaze connected with hers, his eyes darkening as he seemed to read her thoughts. He looked at Katie, his expression pained.

"Several years ago, I was nearly killed in an explosion. In fact, most people believed I did die, from my parents to almost everyone I worked with in the FBI." Scanlon glanced at his wife. "That includes my FBI partner."

"That would be me." Isabel's voice was a soft rasp.

"Isabel had been working on a serial-bomber investigation, and the explosion that nearly killed me was meant for her."

Isabel reached across the picnic table and touched Lacey's arm. "I know what it's like to see someone else take a hit meant for you."

Lacey blinked back tears. "I'm glad for you that Ben survived."

"I didn't know he had for a long time." Isabel reached for her husband's hand, twining her fingers with his. "I felt so guilty and alone."

"When I survived mostly uninjured, the special agent in charge of our team and I agreed it was a perfect opportunity to go undercover in the Swain enclave. I posed as a disgruntled wounded veteran living on disability and looking for some way to make fast, easy money." He looked at Isabel. "Not only did I get a chance to do something active to keep Isabel safe, but I was able to finally remember the truth of what happened the night my father died."

"I don't know how all of this somehow convinces you that J.T. Swain has retired from bomb making," Jim said.

"Like I said, I've been keeping my ear to the ground. And if he's been out there building bombs, he's doing it in the middle of nowhere, with nobody to impress. And that's just not how the Swains do anything."

"What kind of bomb killed your sister?" Isabel asked.

"Honestly, I don't know. The police are keeping some things to themselves on this investigation."

Isabel nodded impatiently. "Do you at least know what kind of detonator was used?"

"Yes, but they don't want this getting out."

"It won't," Ben said firmly.

"The bomb was detonated by a tilt fuse combined with a timer. The timer set the tilt fuse, which then detonated the bomb at the depression of the accelerator."

Ben and Isabel exchanged glances. "Any idea of the explosive material used in the bomb?"

"I'm not sure," Lacey admitted. "That's one of the things the police have held back even from me. But, based on the damage to the car, it seemed to be a small charge directed up into the front seat of the car. It was meant to kill anyone in the passenger-carrying part of the car."

"Any loaded shrapnel?" Isabel asked.

Lacey closed her eyes, wishing she hadn't eaten lunch. Even though Katie was asleep, she lowered her voice. "Ball bearings and sheet-metal screws."

"It's not Swain," Ben and Isabel said in unison.

"How can you know?" Jim asked.

"Needles and nails," Isabel answered. "It's a Swain signature. All their bombs included needles and nails as shrapnel."

"I can't see Jamie setting a bomb without them," Ben agreed.

Lacey leaned closer. "How certain are you about that?"

"Pretty positive. Needles and nails were a matter of pride. It was how the Swains made bombs. To make one without that signature would be like a painter signing someone else's name to his masterpiece."

"That happened, sometimes," Jim murmured.

"Nothing in life is a sure thing," Isabel answered. "But I think Ben is right. There would be needles and nails in that bomb, mixed in with the screws and ball bearings."

"So I guess he goes to the bottom of my suspect list." Lacey tried to quell an overwhelming sense of disappointment. Of the three main suspects she'd settled on, she'd hoped that Swain might be the one who'd killed Marianne and Toby. He was one man, not rich, not particularly powerful, and now that his family members were either in jail or scattered to the winds, he didn't have many allies. Even if he had never been caught, a threat from J.T. Swain would be easier to anticipate and contain.

She felt Jim's fingertips brush her arm, the touch light and tentative. She looked up to find him watching her, his expression concerned.

She moved her arm away from his hand and looked at the Scanlons as she rose to her feet. She extended her hand to Ben. "I appreciate your time. It was generous of you to come out of your way to talk to me."

Ben rose as well and shook her hand. "I wish we could have helped."

By the time they parted company with the Scanlons in the parking lot, the weather conditions were starting to deteriorate, the threat of snow that had followed them into Leesburg finally becoming a reality. Snow fell lightly at first, then in thickening clumps that deteriorated visibility and forced Lacey to slow the Impala to a near crawl only a few miles west of Leesburg.

"Should we stop for a while to see if it slows down?" Jim peered through the windshield at the wall of white flakes. He didn't look worried, exactly, only hypervigilant. Thinking like a bodyguard, she realized.

"I'll feel safer at home than parked out here on the road. It'll be a lot warmer there, too."

The farther they got from Leesburg, the lighter the traffic, which should have made Lacey feel safer. But there was something about the blanket of snow fog that made her feel oddly exposed. The hair on the back of her neck rose, her skin prickling.

Beside her, Jim leaned forward, as if it could help him see farther into the white void only a few yards ahead. They were moving as slowly as Lacey dared, though she didn't want to be going so slowly that a car moving up through the snowfall behind her couldn't stop in time when the driver spotted her taillights.

"This is creepy, isn't it?" she asked. "Like we're all alone in this void."

"We're not alone," Jim growled, turning in his seat to look through the back window.

Lacey checked her rearview mirror. There, emerging through the thick white snow fog behind them, was the now familiar front grille of a blue Toyota Tacoma pickup truck.

Chapter Twelve

"Where the hell did that thing come from?" Lacey's voice rose as she dragged her gaze from the mirror to watch the road ahead. She'd pressed the accelerator on instinct, Jim realized as the Impala picked up speed.

Trying to get away from their pursuer.

He looked behind them, hoping that the truck had dropped back once it spotted the vehicle ahead of it. But it remained close enough that he could almost see past the misting snow and the rapid swish-swish of the truck's windshield wipers.

At first, he didn't quite believe what his eyes were telling him. But after a couple of seconds, the truth sank in. The driver of the blue Tacoma was wearing a ski mask.

Jim slipped his phone from his pocket and dialed Quinn. No point in calling the Virginia State Police. So far, the blue truck's biggest offense was tailgating in a snowstorm. Even if the state police were to respond, by the time they could arrive, whatever the blue pickup had planned would have happened.

He'd carried his Glock on this trip, holstered it inside his jacket. At the moment, the heft of the weapon pressed cold and hard against his rib cage, reminding him that he had options.

Impatiently, he went through the code-phrase rigmarole, then tersely told Quinn what was happening.

"Are you driving?" Quinn asked.

Jim glanced at Lacey, who gripped the steering wheel in two white hands. "No."

"Ms. Miles?"

"Yes."

"Does she have any evasive-driving skills?"

"Do you know anything about evasive driving?" Jim asked Lacey.

"I took a course before I went to Kaziristan a few years ago, but I never had to test what I learned, since I had a driver." She sent another worried glance toward the rearview mirror. "Is that driver wearing a ski mask?"

"Yes."

Lacey made a sound of distress low in her throat. "What should I do?"

"Keep driving," Jim said urgently. "Pick up some speed, but keep your eye on the road ahead." He spoke into the phone again. "So far the truck driver is just keeping pace. Hasn't made a move yet."

"Then just keep moving. Don't go too fast—speed kills," Quinn warned. "I'll see if I can get someone to meet you for an escort."

Jim didn't ask how Quinn would accomplish such a thing. He had come to realize there were few things that his boss couldn't make happen. "I'll be in touch," he told Quinn, then hung up and turned around to look through the back window, half hoping the truck had fallen back.

But, if anything, the front grille of the truck was closer than it had been, bearing down on the back of the Impala like a monster seeking to devour the vehicle and its occupants.

He shifted his gaze to the car seat where Katie still slept, oblivious to the danger that had suddenly engulfed her world in the span of a few heartbeats. A rush of protective affection swamped him, making his head spin for a dizzying moment before his vision cleared and determination steeled his spine.

Katie and Lacey were his to protect, no matter what they or anyone else thought about the matter. If he had to die to protect them, so be it.

Movement in the back window drew his gaze away from Katie's soft face. The truck was pulling up beside the car, its driver's-side front panel aiming for the Impala's rear-side panel.

"PIT maneuver!" Jim shouted, turning to brace himself for the collision.

The truck hit the Impala's right back panel, sending the bulky sport-utility vehicle into a dizzying spin that sent Jim slamming against the passenger door. He kept his head clear of the window, despite the violent jerk of the Impala's rotation.

The car hit a snowy patch and slid across the road toward the ditch on the other side. Lacey steered into the skid and the vehicle came to a stop short of the ditch.

The blue truck had driven past them, disappearing into the white void.

For a long moment, there was nothing but the rumble of the Impala's engine and the hard swish of the windshield wipers. Then a frightened wail rose from the backseat, making Jim's heart skip a beat.

He twisted in his seat until he could see Katie. She was still strapped in her car seat, her eyes crinkled at the corners as she cried.

"It's okay, Katiebug." He searched her visually for any sign of injury. She looked okay, just shaken by the sudden jerks and spins caused by the light impact. "You're okay."

"Are you sure she's okay?" Lacey's voice was a soft rasp beside him.

He turned to look at her. She looked stunned and scared, but he didn't see any sign of an injury on her, either. "She's fine. How about you?"

She lifted her hand to her head. "I hit my head on the window when we took the impact, but it was just a bump. Otherwise, I'm fine. I need to get the car off the road before we get hit."

Jim peered down the road, wondering if the blue truck was waiting just out of sight ahead of them. "Good idea."

Lacey put the car in gear, parked it on the shoulder and engaged the hazard lights. Like Jim, she peered through the whiteout ahead of them. "Do you think he's still up there?"

"Maybe. Now's the time to call the police." He dialed 911 and told the dispatcher what had happened. "We're on VA-9 West. I think we just passed the Loudoun County Animal Shelter a few miles back."

"Is the vehicle that ran you off the road still visible?" the dispatcher asked.

"No, but he could be nearby. The visibility here is bad due to the snow."

"Stay put," the dispatcher said bluntly. "I've got a cruiser headed your way. Anybody injured? You need medical response?"

"No, we're okay," Jim assured her. Even Katie

had stopped crying, save for a few soft sniffles now and then.

"I should get her out of the seat, shouldn't I?" Lacey asked, sounding almost helpless as she looked back at her scared niece.

"No, leave her there. We're off the road, but that doesn't mean we're safe. We all need to stay buckled in and alert." He didn't add that they also needed to keep their eyes peeled for the truck that had run them off the road. He didn't think Lacey needed the reminder.

"Was he trying to make us crash?" she asked a few minutes later as the snow started to fall faster than the windshield wipers could brush the flakes away. "Was that the point? If so, why hasn't he come back for us?"

"I don't know," Jim admitted. "Maybe he was surprised you weren't alone."

"Then why didn't he just drive on without bothering us?"

"Maybe it was too tempting a target to resist." Jim reached across the space between them to cover her hand where it gripped the steering wheel. "The police are on the way. We're all safe."

"Do you have your weapon?" she asked quietly, not pulling her hand away from his grasp.

"Yes."

Her jaw muscle tightened into a knot. "Good."

Moments later, swirling blue lights bled through the snowy void, and a Ford Taurus police interceptor marked with the Virginia State Police insignia loomed into view. The cruiser pulled up behind the Impala on the shoulder and a large black man in a tall black campaign hat and dark blue jacket over a gray uniform stepped from the driver's-side door, approaching the car carefully.

He took their information, including their driver's licenses for routine checks, before he returned to the car and bent to talk to Lacey through the lowered window. "If you think your vehicle can still drive, and you're up for it, I'll escort you to your residence to make sure nothing else happens to disturb your drive."

Jim gave the state policeman a look that didn't quite hide his surprise. "A personal escort home?"

The policeman met his quizzical look with a grim expression. "We don't like it when people get murdered in our state. We're all real sorry for your loss, Ms. Miles. We'd like to make sure you don't suffer any more, so I'll be escorting you home myself."

Jim exchanged a look with Lacey, who smiled at the policeman with genuine gratitude. "Thank you."

The drive home still took longer than it normally would have, since the snow showed little sign of letting up, but eventually, they turned onto the long driveway to the farmhouse without further incident. To Jim's surprise, the state policeman followed them up the drive, parking behind them when they pulled the Impala into the gravel area next to the house.

"I thought I'd take a look around inside, just to be sure nobody's been there while you were gone," said the policeman, whose name badge identified him as Epps. "If you'd like, you can wait out here until I'm done."

"No, we'll come in with you," Lacey said before Jim could insist on the same thing. Epps had been nothing but helpful, but Jim wasn't about to outsource his job of protecting Lacey and Katie to the policeman, however nice and helpful he might be.

Epps looked around the first floor, quickly reassuring himself that there were no signs of forced entry. "Mind if I take a look upstairs?"

"Jim will show you," Lacey said, cuddling Katie close. The little girl was eyeing the big policeman with a combination of wary shyness and curiosity, but she was showing signs of overstimulation, which in Katie led to tantrums. "I'll settle Katie down to finish her nap."

Jim left them reluctantly and joined Epps on

the stairs. The policeman sidled a look Jim's way when he encountered the locked door.

"Ms. Miles's office. She's working from home these days, and since her reports can often deal in proprietary information..."

"Right," Epps said, not sounding convinced by Jim's explanation but apparently deciding it was none of his business. "I don't know that it'll help much for you to give your statements on what happened if you didn't get the license plate of the truck that hit you, but I'll be happy to file a report, in case we can track down the vehicle."

"Good idea," Jim agreed, and when they returned to the first floor, he and Lacey took turns telling Epps what they could remember about the vehicle that had tried to run them off the road.

"Ski mask?" Epps's dark eyebrows rose when Jim described what he'd seen.

"I know it sounds strange."

"I reckon *strange* is a relative thing when someone's already set a car bomb to take you out." Epps finished taking the report and got Jim to sign his statement. "We'll be in touch."

Jim locked the door behind Epps and headed down the hall to Katie's room, where he found Lacey rocking her niece slowly in the rocking chair next to the crib. Katie was asleep, but Lacey showed no signs of letting the little girl go.

"It wasn't the same truck, was it?" she asked as Jim leaned against the door frame.

"I don't think so," he admitted. "It didn't hit me until I was telling Epps about the PIT maneuver. The blue truck we saw in the bomb-scene video had that dent in the driver's-side front panel. The truck that hit us this afternoon didn't."

"Probably does now," Lacey murmured, bleak humor in her voice. "I'm not sure what it means that it was a different truck. Any thoughts?"

"Maybe he bought a new truck."

"Same as the old truck?"

Jim shook his head. "Not likely, is it?"

"Maybe it's a different person," Lacey suggested. "But someone who wants us to think it's the same blue truck that's been following me."

Jim pulled the tufted ottoman that matched the rocker closer to where Lacey sat. His legs were far too long for the small footrest, but he perched there as well as he could and settled his gaze on Lacey and the sleeping child, his heart pounding a little harder at the memory of how close he'd come to losing them both that day.

"What would be the point of making us think it's the other truck?" he asked softly, unable to keep from reaching out to touch the velvet curve of Katie's cheek.

"I'm not sure," Lacey admitted. "Maybe to lead us off track? Misdirection of some sort?"

Jim dropped his hand away from Katie's face. "Focus us in one direction so we don't see trouble coming from another one?"

"Maybe." Lacey's fingers followed the path Jim's had traced along Katie's plump cheek. "There's a more pertinent question, though."

He watched the slow glide of her fingers over Katie's skin, wishing she would reach across the space between them and touch him with that same tenderness.

Not that tenderness was all he wanted from her. Not by a long shot.

But he'd ruined his chances for more. It was time he learned to accept that fact.

"What question?" he asked when Lacey didn't immediately continue.

"I haven't told many people about the truck," she said quietly. "You know, of course, but I don't think you'd do anything to put Katie—or me—in danger."

"God, no."

"Your boss, but the same applies. They'd have no reason to put us in danger that way."

"Which leaves whom?"

"Detective Bolling at the Arlington County

Police Department, and Detective Miller with the DC Metro Police. I told both of them about the truck. But nobody else."

"What about the cop in Frederick? You told me you saw the blue truck following you that day. Did you mention it to that detective?"

"No, I didn't. I'm sure I didn't, because I remember thinking later that day that I should have mentioned it, but I didn't."

"So you think our copycat truck driver was a cop?"

"Or someone one of those cops told about it."

Jim frowned, not liking the implications. Protecting Lacey and Katie was hard enough with the cops on his side. But if one of them was working with the enemy...

"This seems like something the Whittiers would pull," Lacey said bluntly. "Maybe the point is to scare me, keep me so tangled up in the threats against me that I'm not poking my nose into their business."

"It's certainly not the sort of thing al Adar would bother with," Jim agreed. "But compared to a car bomb, what that truck did today is pretty mild."

"If he'd succeeded in driving us completely off the road, it could have been much worse. We could have been killed."

"I don't mean that what he did to us wasn't

dangerous. Of course it was. But it wasn't a sure thing, the way that bomb was." He frowned, his mind racing through the possibilities. "If you really think about it, everything that's happened since the bombing has been weak in comparison. The mugging in Frederick. The truck following you all over DC."

"Ken Calvert was murdered," Lacey pointed out. "That's not exactly a downgrade."

"If his death was connected to what's been happening to you," Jim said. "We don't know that it was anything more than a mugging gone tragically wrong."

"It would be a hell of a coincidence."

"But coincidences do happen."

Lacey rose from the rocking chair, forcing Jim to rise as well and pull the ottoman out of her way. She carried Katie to the crib and gently laid her on the mattress, stroking Katie's hair when she stirred until the little girl drifted back to sleep. Putting her finger to her lips, she motioned for Jim to lead the way out of the nursery.

They ended up in the kitchen, facing each other across the table. Outside, artificial twilight had fallen with the snow, reflecting their images back at them in the windowpanes.

"Maybe we've been going about this all wrong," Lacey said, resting her chin on her palm as she gazed wearily across the table at Jim.

"How's that?"

"We've assumed it's just one person after me. But I had three suspects."

"One of which we're pretty sure we eliminated today after talking to the Scanlons."

"But that still leaves two parties with a reason to want me out of the way." Lacey rose and crossed to the counter, coming to a stop in front of the coffeemaker. After a brief hesitation, she opened a cabinet, pulled out filters and a can of dark roast, and set about brewing a fresh pot of coffee.

Jim watched her going through the motions, realizing that she was one of those people who thought best when she was in action. He could almost see the wheels turning in her brain, moving in concert with her busy hands.

"I think whoever was driving the original blue truck, the one that showed up at the scene of the car bomb and later followed me to Frederick and then DC, has one agenda. The person in the truck today had another one." She finished filling the coffeemaker with water and turned to face him, looking as if she'd lost her train of thought when she finished her task of putting on a pot of coffee to brew.

"I agree," he said, rising to join her at the counter. "You hungry? I could use a snack."

"I'll get it," she said quickly, already heading for the refrigerator. "Cheese and fruit?"

"Perfect." He opened the cabinet and pulled out a couple of mugs for their coffee. "I've been thinking about the suspects on your list, and the ones who make the most sense, in terms of having access to police information and the means by which to produce a nearly identical truck, have to be the Whittiers."

She had gathered a bunch of grapes, a small bag of cherries and a couple of navel oranges from the refrigerator and deposited them on the counter by the sink. "They'd definitely have the means to come up with a blue pickup," she agreed as she started washing the fruit. "But that also suggests maybe they're not the ones who arranged for the bomb in my car, doesn't it?"

"Because of the de-escalation of attacks?"

"Exactly. The first strike was a deadly car bomb that would have killed me had I been driving that night." Her hands faltered as she pulled a clean cloth from a nearby drawer and laid the freshly washed fruit on the cloth to dry. "But the things that happened after that seem more like attempts to scare me rather than kill me. Like the mugger that day in Frederick. He could have shot me rather than tried to grab me. I had thought maybe he wanted to get me alone and start asking me questions, and maybe he did. But even that could have been meant to scare me."

"Maybe the blue truck that followed you that day really did have nothing to do with the mugger."

She retrieved a block of Havarti cheese from the crisper, carried it to the counter and started slicing. "Maybe not." She put down her knife suddenly, turning to look at him. "But if the guy in the blue truck set the bomb that killed Marianne and Toby, why hasn't he made another real attempt on my life?"

Chapter Thirteen

"How did you get these?" Lacey looked with skepticism at the pair of Quik-Trak train tickets Jim had set on the kitchen table at breakfast the next morning.

"Quinn had someone drop them by last night. You were already asleep."

She frowned. "Why does he think we should go to Connecticut? What will it accomplish?"

Jim sat beside Katie's high chair, retrieving a piece of orange that had escaped the baby's sticky grasp and landed on the table. "If nothing else, it'll change the paradigm."

"What does that even mean?" Lacey picked up the tickets and read the details. "Jim, this train leaves before seven tomorrow morning."

"I know. We need to start packing."

She felt rebellion rising in her chest. This was happening too fast and was completely out of her control. A man named Alexander Quinn had decided a trip to Connecticut to meet with the elusive Whittier brothers was in order, and suddenly she was holding two tickets on the train from Union Station to the station in Stamford, Connecticut, which was the closest town to the coastal Whittier family compound. "I need to think about this, Jim."

"I know I've just thrown this at you without any notice, but I think Quinn is right. We're sitting ducks out here, waiting for things to happen to us." He reached across the table and put his hand over hers. She felt a warm shock, as if he'd touched a live wire to her skin. Her fingers tingled in response, even though she knew the electric sensation was all in her head. "That's not the way I like to live my life. I don't think that's the way you like to live yours, either."

She wanted to argue with him, but on that subject, at least, he was right. She was a risk taker, an envelope pusher. She made things happen rather than waiting for things to happen to her.

"How are we supposed to convince the Whittiers to talk to us?"

"Quinn said he was working on that."

"So we go there without any plan?"

"It's better than sitting here twiddling our thumbs."

"What about Katie?" She forced herself to

pull her hand from his warm, gentle grasp. She was letting herself get too close to him again, letting herself feel more than she wanted to, more than was safe.

"Remember the family I worked for, the Becketts? They've agreed to come out here to the farm for a couple of days to take care of Katie. They have a six-year-old daughter named Samantha, who will love spending a couple of days with Katie."

"I don't know these people."

"But I do." He leaned closer to her, capturing her gaze. "I would never do anything to put Katie in danger. I know you don't trust me anymore, and maybe you never will again. But you have to know at least that much about me. Don't you?"

His gaze ensnared her, blazing with the truth. He might have lied to her about who he really was and why he was there at the farmhouse with her and Katie, but she believed with every fiber of her being that he would take a bullet for her or Katie. "I know you'd never do anything to hurt her," she admitted softly.

"Cade Beckett is a retired Navy SEAL with more awards and commendations than you could fit on the wall of your office upstairs. His wife, Julie, was an FBI agent before she decided she was missing too much of her daughter's life and decided to take a consulting job with the Kentucky Bureau of Investigation so she could stay home with Samantha."

"They're willing to drop everything for a couple of days to babysit Katie?"

"Cade works for Campbell Cove Security. Coming here to stay with Katie is sort of his job. Julie works from home via computer, which she can do just as easily from here, as long as the Wi-Fi holds up. And she homeschools Samantha."

She looked at him through narrowed eyes, wondering if she was being played a little bit. "You have this all figured out."

"It wasn't my idea. That was all Quinn. But the more I think about it, the better I like it. I'm not sure it's good for Katie to be stuck out here with only us for companionship. Having Samantha around to play with her for a couple of days could be a good thing for Katie, as well."

"And meanwhile, we're standing at the gates of the Whittier compound yelling *Here we are, come get us*?"

"That's not exactly how I'd put it," Jim protested.

"But it's pretty close to how it will be, isn't it?" she asked, automatically picking up a napkin to wipe the orange juice from Katie's fingers before the little girl started to rub her drooping eyes. Funny, she realized, how she'd somehow transitioned from hapless aunt to practiced mother figure without even noticing it had happened.

She wasn't Katie's mother. She'd never be that, not really. She'd always make sure her niece knew all about Marianne and Toby, thought of them as her parents and never forgot she was their daughter.

But, for all intents and purposes, Lacey was truly Katie's parent now, and it had happened without her realizing it.

The urge to cry was suddenly overwhelming. She rose quickly to her feet and crossed to the window over the sink, gazing out at the snowy backyard as she fought against the tears beating at the backs of her eyes.

Behind her, she could hear the sounds of Jim taking charge of Katie, extracting her from the high chair and wiping up the remains of her breakfast of oatmeal and orange slices. When she brought her emotions back under control, she turned to watch him finish wiping orange juice from Katie's sticky hands with a wet cloth and lower the little girl to the floor.

"I'm going to take her outside to make another snowman," Jim said quietly, clearly pretending he hadn't noticed Lacey's struggle with her emotions. "I left the phone number for the

Becketts on the table in the parlor in case you didn't keep my résumé. You may want to give them a call and talk to them yourself before you decide what to do."

"Thank you."

He gave a shrug as if to say it was no problem and herded Katie out of the kitchen.

She found the number Jim left for her and made the call. She had spoken to Cade Beckett when she'd called to check Jim's references, but this time, it was a woman who answered the phone. In the background, Lacey could hear a little girl laughing.

"Mrs. Beckett? This is Lacey Miles. Jim Mercer works for me as a nanny." Among other things.

"Oh, yes! He said you'd be calling." Julie Beckett's voice was low and warm, with just a hint of the Midwest in her accent. "He's told you about what Alexander Quinn proposed?"

"He did, but I'm not sure why you and your husband agreed."

"Because Jim told us about your situation. I'm sorry for your loss."

Unexpected tears pricked Lacey's eyes. Julie Beckett sounded genuinely sympathetic. "Thank you."

"Quinn told us you and Jim need to go out of

town for a couple of days to investigate a lead, and you need someone to watch your niece."

"Yes. Katie's two. She can be a handful, and I don't want to put her in any more dangerous situations."

"I understand completely." Julie's voice softened as if she could sense Lacey's sudden vulnerability through the phone line. "I can give you references. For my FBI work, anyway."

"What field office?"

"Louisville for the past five years. I spent my rookie years at a variety of field offices and resident agencies."

Lacey knew an agent in the Louisville field office. She'd give him a call later this morning. "When do you plan to get here?"

"It's about a seven-hour drive, so we were hoping to get on the road early today. Do we need to bring air beds? Samantha loves camping, so it wouldn't be a big deal if we need to rough it a little."

"It's a huge house with six bedrooms. I'll air out a couple of rooms for you." Was she really agreeing to having strangers come into her house and stay with her niece?

Yes, a treacherous little voice answered, *because they're Jim's friends and he trusts them.*

"I'm looking forward to meeting you. I'm a

big fan of your reporting, and Jim speaks so highly of you."

"He speaks well of you, too. We'll have rooms ready for you when you arrive. I'll go shopping, too, so you'll have plenty of food in the pantry. Any food allergies I should know about?"

"No, we'll eat anything!" Julie laughed.

They worked through a few logistics before they hung up, and, despite her earlier misgivings, Lacey had begun to agree with Jim that having the Becketts come to the farm to watch Katie just might be a good idea.

BY THE TIME Cade and Julie Beckett arrived with their daughter, Samantha, Lacey and Jim had managed to wash and dry fresh linens for the guest bedrooms, and Jim had made a trip into town to pick up groceries.

Jim was looking forward to seeing the Becketts again, especially Samantha. He'd received a few letters and cards from her and the Becketts since he'd left their employ, but it wasn't the same as seeing them every day. He'd jumped in when their previous nanny quit to get married, and he'd begun to feel as if he was part of the family. While he'd understood Julie's decision to work from home so she could be with Samantha, he hadn't been happy about looking for a new job.

"When I left the Marine Corps," he confessed to Lacey over lunch, "I was at loose ends. I had joined up thinking it was a life about as far from my crazy, close-knit family as I could get, and at that time in my life, I guess, that was the escape I'd needed. But after a few years, I knew that I wouldn't be happy doing that kind of work. I missed being part of a family. My own brother and sisters are all grown up, and while we see each other on holidays, it's not the same."

"You thought working with children would help you recapture that feeling?" Lacey observed him over the rim of her coffee cup, her gray eyes sharp, making him feel as if she were trying to read the emotions behind his words. It was a disconcerting sensation but also a strangely welcome one. Her curiosity suggested she wanted to know what made him tick.

Maybe that was a good sign. If she cared what he thought, maybe she could eventually forgive his lies of omission.

"I thought it might. It didn't really fill in all the gaps in my life, but it did make me realize that what I'd been running from when I joined the Marine Corps was the life I really want. A home. Wife and kids and maybe a dog in the backyard or a cat or two."

Lacey's lips curved in the first genuine smile

he'd seen from her in what seemed like days. "Domestic bliss?"

"More like the knowledge that there's somewhere in the world you belong, no matter how far you roam."

A suspicious brightness glittered in her eyes, and she blinked a couple of times as if to keep tears from forming. Her gaze settled on her niece's face. "Katie is that for me now. You know?"

Katie looked up at Lacey and grinned around her bite of cheese sandwich, making Lacey laugh.

"I know," he said, reaching across the table to cover her hand with his. She didn't pull away. Progress. "Julie and Cade will take good care of her. They're both trained to handle dangerous situations. She couldn't be in better hands. And she'll love playing with Samantha."

"Mantha!" Katie repeated with another big grin. Jim and Lacey had prepared her for the arrival of their visitors, and she was almost as excited to see the Becketts as Jim was.

The phone rang as she and Jim were cleaning up the kitchen after lunch. It was Detective Miller of the DC Metro Police. "I thought you'd want to know, we've made an arrest in the Ken Calvert murder case."

Lacey gripped the phone more tightly, looking across the kitchen at Jim. "Who killed him?"

"His ex-wife. She confessed an hour ago to hiring someone to shoot him. They were tangled up in a custody battle over their two kids, and it looks like the ex–Mrs. Calvert decided killing him was easier than coming to some sort of agreement."

"My God. How awful."

"Yeah, ain't love grand?" Miller's flat tone suggested he'd seen too many senseless murders in the course of his police career. "Thought you'd want to know."

"Thanks for calling." She hung up and turned to Jim. "It looks like Ken Calvert's murder really was a coincidence. His ex-wife hired someone to kill him. She just confessed."

"My dad used to say, always look at the spouse first." Jim folded the dish towel he'd used to wipe the table and laid it on the counter. "Well, at least it's one loose end tied up."

"Yeah, but poor Ken. And those poor kids." Lacey looked at Katie, who was sitting in the corner of the kitchen, trying to get the top off her empty sippy cup. "The death of a parent is never fair to the kids."

"Yeah," Jim said with a sigh. "I know."

"But I still don't know what Ken was going to tell me." She sighed. "What if it was important?"

Jim put his hand on her shoulder, leveling his gaze with her. "Then we'll find out another way."

The Becketts arrived a little after three that afternoon, rumpled from the long drive but smiling as soon as they saw Jim in the open doorway. After a round of hugs, Jim introduced them to Lacey and Katie.

Julie was a tall, slim woman with a shoulder-length bob of shiny dark hair and eyes the color of black coffee. She spoke with a soft Midwest accent and was quick with a smile. Her husband, Cade, was tall, fit and quiet, with sharp blue eyes beneath a rusty buzz cut that made him look as if he was fresh out of boot camp.

As expected, Samantha and Katie took to each other immediately, heading outside with Cade to play in the snow that lingered in the yard from the snowfall the day before.

Julie stayed behind, happily accepting a cup of hot chocolate at the kitchen table. "Anything new happen while we were on the road?"

"No, just handling all the last-minute details." Jim glanced at Lacey. She met his gaze calmly enough, but he could see thoughts sparking behind her eyes. This must be what she looked like when she sniffed out a hot new story, he thought. Part excited, part anxious and part pure, gritty nerve.

"There's a guy I know in Stamford," Julie said in a casual tone that Jim knew was anything but casual. "His name is Mickey Grimes, and he used to be in the Bureau. He left the FBI a few years ago, but if there's anybody in Connecticut who can get you a meeting with one of the Whittier brothers, it's Mickey."

Lacey apparently picked up the undertones in Julie's words. "He left the FBI...of his own volition?"

"He was encouraged to retire early." Julie shrugged one shoulder. "He's not squeaky clean, but he's also not a monster. He's been working security for Justin Whittier for the past couple of years. He's loyal to Whittier, but his loyalty doesn't extend to condoning murder."

"Are you sure?"

"Yes." Julie took a long sip of her hot chocolate, as if she was carefully considering her next words. "I know you think that the Whittiers are being treated as untouchables, but the FBI was investigating them both at the time I left the Bureau. There are details I'm not at liberty to share with you, but I can tell you this much. Of the two brothers, Carson is the wild card. Justin has secrets, but they're personal, not criminal. And from a few things Mickey let drop the last time I talked to him, I think Justin may be getting a little tired of being lumped in with his brother's misadventures."

"So if Mickey could get us a face-to-face meeting with Justin Whittier…" Jim began.

"He might be willing to tell you whether or not the threats against you are coming from his family. Just to get it off his chest." Julie set her cup down on the table in front of her. "I'd better go see what my crew is up to," she said with a smile that belied the seriousness of the previous conversation. She gave Jim's shoulder an affectionate pat and headed out to retrieve her coat from the mudroom.

"I like her," Lacey said bluntly.

"I knew you would." Jim gathered up the empty hot-chocolate cups and put them in the dishwasher. "She was a real go-getter in the FBI. Driven to succeed. Reminds me of you."

"That's how you see me?" Lacey gave him a thoughtful look. "A go-getter, driven to succeed?"

"Isn't that what you are?" He leaned his hips against the kitchen counter, folded his arms over his chest and met her gaze. "It's not a bad thing."

"Julie left that life behind to be with her daughter."

"She did."

"Nobody at my office expects me to do that for Katie, you know." She stood and crossed to the window over the sink, close enough that Jim could feel the warmth of her body wafting over him. She gazed out at the backyard, where the Becketts and Katie were finishing up a small lopsided snowman. It had taken nearly all of the two-inch snowfall in the yard to build, but Katie wouldn't be denied. "They're surprised I haven't already returned to work, if you want to know the truth. I can hear it in their voices when I call in for my messages. They're confused and worried that I haven't met their expectations."

"Do you think you're ready to go back?"

She shook her head. "I thought I'd be climbing the walls here by the end of the first week, but it's turned out to be much more comfortable than I'd anticipated. I've had my own investigation into the car bombing to keep me occupied, of course. I suppose that might be part of the reason I haven't been as restless as I thought I'd be. But I don't miss the hustle and bustle of the newsroom, and I really thought I would."

"I don't miss the Marine Corps the way I thought I would, either. Change is constant, and it doesn't have to be a bad thing."

Lacey gave him another thoughtful look, then turned back to the window, her gaze following Katie as the little girl ran ecstatic circles around the off-kilter snowman.

THE TRAIN ARRIVED in Stamford on time, shortly before noon. On the busy concourse, a stocky man with thinning black hair stood with a sign that read "Jim Mercer."

Lacey pointed out the man to Jim as they grabbed their overnight cases. "That must be Mickey Grimes." At Jim's request, Julie Beckett had called Grimes to set up a meeting with him once they arrived in Stamford. Instead, Grimes had insisted on meeting their train.

"Do you think we're crazy to trust him?"

"I'm not sure I'd call this trust," Jim murmured, draping the canvas strap of his overnight bag over his shoulder. "But Grimes has access to the Whittiers. We need that access."

Grimes flashed a friendly smile when he spotted their approach. But Lacey perceived a certain wariness there as well, as if he realized he was walking a thin edge between honest work and illegal activity. When they were close enough, he spoke in a quiet tone. "Justin Whittier is waiting in his limousine. He wants to speak to you. But I have to search you for weapons and wires before he'll talk to you. He's arranged for a room where we can conduct the search."

"That's out of the question." Jim's tone was tight with fury.

Lacey put a hand on his arm. "I'm willing to meet that requirement."

Jim looked at her, frustration seething in his hazel-green eyes. Whatever he saw in her expression seemed to calm his anger, for he simply nodded.

The room Grimes took them to looked to be little more than a closet a few dozen yards down the concourse from where they'd exited the train. Grimes entered first, took a quick look around as if to ensure that they were alone, then nodded for them to follow.

Inside, the room was crowded and smelled of antiseptic. Bottles on a shelf at the back of the room suggested it might be a place where the train station stored cleaning supplies.

"Either of you armed?"

"No," Jim answered.

"Lift your shirts."

Lacey did so without hesitation. She had gone through more humiliating searches during her reporting career, conducted by men who were far less businesslike about the process.

Jim grimaced as he showed Grimes he wasn't wearing a wire. "Does Justin Whittier require this sort of degradation from everyone he talks to?"

Grimes didn't answer. "Let's go.

They followed him out of the station to a

long black limousine parked in what should have been a no-parking zone. But if the security personnel at the Amtrak station had noticed, they showed no sign of trying to move the vehicle along. There was a driver standing outside the passenger compartment doors, apparently awaiting their arrival.

"You can leave your bags here. Jaffe will watch them for you," Grimes said as they reached the vehicle.

Reluctantly, Lacey set her bag on the curb in front of the driver. Jim did the same as Grimes opened the car door and waved them into the limo.

Jim went first, pausing for a moment, blocking the door. After a moment, he continued into the car, turning to give Lacey a warning look.

"In," Grimes said firmly when she considered making a run for it.

Reluctantly, she stepped into the limousine and sat next to Jim, who was staring at the occupants of the bench seat opposite them. Lacey found herself face-to-face with Justin Whittier and another man she'd never seen before. But what arrested her attention about the stranger was the bruise on his cheek that matched almost perfectly the bruise on her own cheek where she'd hit the window of the SUV when the blue truck had tried to run them off the road.

"Ms. Miles, a pleasure to finally meet you," Justin Whittier said smoothly. He had a cultured, easy tone, nearly accent-free, and if he found anything worrisome about this impromptu meeting, he hid it well.

"I think we both know this has nothing to do with pleasure," she said flatly. Beside her, Jim's body felt tightly sprung, as if he was just waiting to jump into action. She hoped that wouldn't be necessary.

"Perhaps not. Nevertheless, I want to make an apology on behalf of my brother, Carson. I believe he may have been involved in the accident you had a couple of days ago."

Chapter Fourteen

Justin Whittier looked sincerely apologetic, but Jim knew better than to take anyone, especially a politician, at face value.

"Can you be more specific about your brother's involvement in the accident?" he asked, his voice taut with rising anger. Who the hell did this man think he was, pulling a stunt like this? Did he think the show of power and wealth would impress him or Lacey in the slightest?

Maybe he was used to getting what he wanted just by waving a few bills or favors in people's faces. It had gotten him this far, apparently.

"Carson's involvement was, I'd like to assure you, entirely inadvertent. I'd like to apologize for my brother's judgment in employees, for one thing." Whittier looked at the man sitting beside him. "Morris? Would you like to tell Ms. Miles what you did?"

The man named Morris slanted a furious look

at Whittier before he schooled his features—though not without visible effort—into a look of regret. "Mr. Whittier asked me to find a way to discourage you from continuing your investigation into his congressional run," Morris said in a meek tone that Jim was pretty sure he'd never used before. His accent was pure Brooklyn, and his bulky build suggested he might have been hired more for his muscle than any particular talent.

Lacey nodded toward his bruise. "You drove the Toyota Tacoma that ran us off the road the other day."

Morris's only answer was a grudging nod.

"Morris has, of course, been released from my brother's employ, and we will be happy to pay for any repairs to your vehicle and other costs incurred, with the understanding that our name must never be connected to the payment."

"There's no need. I can't be bought," Lacey said flatly. "In lieu of the payment, I'd like a truthful answer to one question—who told Mr. Morris to drive a blue Toyota Tacoma to run me off the road?"

Whittier looked honestly puzzled, and for once, Jim was inclined to believe him. He looked at Morris, who turned his gaze to Mickey Grimes.

"I'm afraid that might be my doing," Grimes

said ruefully. "See, I have a friend in the Arlington County police department, and he told me about the video of one of the Whittier limos passing by the crime scene the night of the car bombing."

"Forgive me," Whittier interrupted. "I should have said this earlier. I am truly sorry for your loss. I lost a younger brother when I was in my teens, and it was a devastating blow. I can sympathize with your grief."

"Thank you," Lacey said, her voice tight with impatience. She turned to look at Grimes. "You were saying about the limousine?"

"My friend in Arlington wondered if I could tell him why one of the Whittiers was in the area that night, and I explained that Mr. Carson had a meeting with some donors nearby that evening. He accepted my answer and told me it was a formality. It seems the police were a little more interested in a blue Toyota Tacoma that was also in the area and was believed to be following you around since the bombing."

"And you shared this information with Morris?" Jim asked through gritted teeth.

"Well, Mr. Carson, actually, but Morris was there."

"I thought it would distract you, send you looking in another direction rather than bothering Mr. Carson and Mr. Justin all the time,"

Morris growled, looking less and less apologetic by the minute.

"Please accept my apology on behalf of my brother and his former employee," Whittier said. "You could have been badly hurt by his idiotic stunt, and I'm deeply grateful that you seem to have incurred no lasting damage."

Lacey was silent a moment, but Jim could feel the vibration of her anger sending tremors through her slim body. She finally spoke, in a voice rattling with rage. "My two-year-old niece was in that vehicle, Mr. Whittier. She could have easily been hurt or even killed. What your brother's employee did, no doubt with your brother's approval, could have resulted in first-degree murder. Do you understand that? Do you even care?"

"I assure you, my brother knew nothing of Morris's plans. Morris will not receive any further payment from anyone in my family, nor will he receive any sort of recommendation for future employment, and if asked, we will certainly inform potential employers of his reckless lack of judgment."

"What about the attack in Frederick?" Lacey asked.

Jim looked at her, surprised. She was looking at Morris, her gaze narrowed. He held her gaze, anger in his eyes, but he said nothing.

"What attack in Frederick?" Justin Whittier seemed genuinely surprised.

"Your brother's associate here—"

"Ex-associate," Whittier corrected.

"Whoever. He's the man who attacked me in Frederick."

Jim stared at her, wondering if she was bluffing. But she looked utterly confident in what she was saying.

"You see, he may have been wearing a mask, but when I hit him with the tire iron from my trunk, he let fly a stream of invective that would have made a longshoreman blush. He had a rather distinctive voice. With a Brooklyn accent."

Whittier shot a black look at Morris before he looked back at Lacey with an expression so bland Jim almost thought he'd imagined the previous anger he'd seen in the man's face.

"I'm sure you must be mistaken. Is that the only evidence you can supply of Morris's alleged involvement in an attack on you?"

Lacey's lips pressed into a thin line that Jim knew meant she was pissed, but she merely nodded.

"Well, you can see the dilemma, then. Despite our conversation here today, there is no evidence that Morris was involved in the attack on you in Frederick, or that he caused your unfortunate accident. My brother and I have no knowledge of the whereabouts or even the existence of the blue Tacoma in question. You can see the difficulty in pursuing legal charges against Morris, since I'm certain that Morris will not be so willing to tell the police what he told you today."

Morris muttered a profane agreement.

"My hands are tied, legally at least. This is the best reparation I can offer you, and I do so at some risk, considering your career as a journalist. I am hoping that you understand the need for discretion, as you have no evidence to back up anything you might want to share about this situation."

"She has me as a witness," Jim said bluntly.

Justin Whittier turned his cool blue gaze to Jim. "Yes. Ms. Miles's recently employed nanny." He spoke the last word with a touch of pure disdain, which did nothing to cool the anger rising in Jim's chest.

"And a decorated Marine Corps sergeant with connections to a lot of people in high places," he snapped, leveling his gaze with Whittier's.

For a second, Whittier's placid facade slipped, revealing a look of alarm and, quick on its heels, anger. But he quickly brought his expression back under control. "What exactly do you propose?"

"Mutual assured destruction. Of a sort." Jim

leaned a little closer to Whittier, using his size and his gritty anger as a weapon of intimidation.

Next to Lacey, Grimes started to move toward the escalating confrontation, but Lacey grabbed his arm, holding him in place. She nodded at Jim to continue.

"We have the information we need about what happened on that snowy road in Virginia. And the added information about what happened in Frederick. If any further threat arises from your family or their employees, we will not hesitate to tell the police everything we know, including your attempt to bribe us into silence."

"That was *not* a bribe attempt," Justin protested.

Jim ignored him. "In exchange for your promise that no harm or trouble will come Ms. Miles's way from your family and associates, we will not share this information with the authorities."

"What about Ms. Miles's investigation into my family's affairs?"

Jim shrugged. "I am not authorized to make any promises to that end."

"I am a reporter," Lacey said flatly. "If you or your family makes news, I am obligated to report it and to do so thoroughly and without prejudice. I will make no promises that would impede me from doing so."

Justin looked at her through narrowed eyes as if considering her words carefully. Finally, his expression cleared, and he nodded. "Fair enough. It is my hope that Carson has learned his lesson about his choices for employees." His voice grew steely. "If not, he is on his own."

"Are we done here?" Jim asked, looking not at Justin Whittier but at Mickey Grimes.

Stone-faced, Grimes nodded. He opened the door of the limousine and stepped out, allowing them to disembark, as well. He gave a polite nod to the driver, who opened the driver's door and slid in behind the steering wheel. Grimes stepped back into the limousine, gave Jim and Lacey a parting salute, and closed the door just as the limousine pulled away from the curb.

Jim looked down at the luggage at his feet and blew out a long breath. "Well, that was deeply dissatisfying."

Lacey lifted her bag, swinging the strap over her shoulder. "I don't know. It answered a lot of questions and kept us from chasing those particular wild geese." She nodded toward the concourse. "We could exchange our tickets for tomorrow's train for one this afternoon. Cancel our hotel reservations and be back in Cherry Grove by dinnertime."

"We could," he agreed. "Or we could find a nice restaurant here in town, get some lunch and maybe use this baby-free time to revise and rework your suspect list."

She looked at him through narrowed eyes, as if weighing her options with care. Finally, the furrows that creased her brow disappeared, and she smiled. "It might be nice to be able to brainstorm this investigation without having to stop every few minutes to tend to a toddler." Immediately she looked guilty. "God, that sounded terrible. I adore Katie, you know I do."

He put his hands on her shoulders, bending toward her. "I do know. But you're right. It's nice to have a break from being a parent. And it's good for Katie, too, to be interacting with people outside her immediate family. So don't feel guilty. Take advantage of the break to reconnect with who you are outside of Katie."

She cocked her head. "Did you get that out of some child-rearing self-help book?"

He grinned. "Maybe."

She let out a long sigh and smiled back. "There's supposed to be an amazing sushi place on Main Street. How do you feel about raw fish?"

"Not quite as adventurous as some of the things I ate in Afghanistan, but I'm game."

Lacey nodded toward the taxi stand a few yards down the concourse. "Then let's hail a cab, stash our bags at the hotel and go eat some sushi."

THE NEREID LIVED UP to the rave reviews a couple of Lacey's fellow reporters had given it. The sushi rolls were fresh and delicious, and the miso soup was as close to the homemade miso soup she'd consumed on her last trip to Japan as she'd tasted on this side of the globe.

The company wasn't bad, either. They'd been shown to a table near the restaurant's glass front, and the afternoon sunlight slanting through the windows bathed Jim's face in golden light that seemed to highlight just what an attractive man he was.

Pretending she didn't find him nearly irresistible was only making things worse for her, she knew. She'd drop her guard and then he'd say something or do something or, hell, just look at her a particular way and she'd be gut punched by just how tempting a man he really was.

But she couldn't trust him. She couldn't. He'd come into her life on the basis of a lie and hadn't told her the truth until it was clear he'd been found out. What kind of basis was that for any sort of honest, sustainable relationship?

And in what position was she these days to have any sort of relationship with any man? She was still grieving her sister, still trying to sort out the tatters of her life, trying to figure out how to be a mother to her orphaned niece. What man would want to be part of that upheaval?

Jim, a treacherous voice in her head whispered. *Jim would want to be part of that upheaval.*

"There's that little crease," Jim said, looking at her over a cup of hot tea. The delicate porcelain cup looked ridiculously out of place in his big hand, but he didn't seem to notice the incongruity.

"What crease?" she asked, trying not to remember how gentle those big, strong hands could be when he touched her.

"The one between your eyebrows. It means you're worrying about something you can't figure out." He sat back in his chair, setting the cup on the table. "So, want to tell Uncle Jim what's bothering you?"

"Just this mess Katie and I are in," she lied. It should be what was bothering her instead of what she wanted to do about her ridiculous crush on Jim Mercer.

"Take an hour's break from all that. You're in lovely Stamford, Connecticut, with nothing pressing to do until seven tomorrow morning."

"What are you suggesting? That we take a drive down to Cove Island Park and take a bunch of selfies to send to our families and friends?"

"Interesting that Cove Island Park is where

your mind went immediately. Ever been there?" he asked.

She shook her head. "No. Have you?"

"Yes, actually." His smile softened with the memory. "I was maybe four years into my Marine Corps career, and my little sister Jen was a junior at Yale. At the time, I was assigned to a ship that had docked in the New York Harbor during Fleet Week. Jen had just finished her final exams and was planning to join a friend the next week for a trip to London and Paris, so it was our only chance to see each other. A buddy of mine who had family in the Bronx talked them into letting me borrow a car to drive to Stamford so I could meet Jen halfway. She packed a picnic and we spent the day in Cove Island Park, catching up on each other's lives." He sighed, some of the softness in his expression fading into melancholy. "Kids. They don't call, they don't write…"

"Where is Jen now?"

"Happily married to a brilliant surgeon at Johns Hopkins. Which she also happens to be. She's the poster child for success." His smile of pride was downright incandescent. "She calls every week or two, just to rub it in."

Lacey laughed. "What about the others?"

"Richard is a graphic designer for an ad agency in Knoxville, Tennessee, where he attended college. Huge Tennessee fan, which is bearable only because his beloved Vols and my beloved Tar Heels are in two different football conferences." He smiled. "And Hallie just got her master's in genetics from Princeton and is about to start her doctoral classes at Harvard. Thank God for full scholarships, huh?"

"You come from a family of overachievers, apparently."

Jim grinned. "I do. They make me look like a total slacker. At least my mom thinks I'm brilliant and perfect."

Lacey smiled. "Sounds like maybe you are. Your brother and sisters got where they are because of you. You're the one who stepped in when they needed someone to be their parent, even though you were just a kid yourself. You gave them the love and support they needed to fly."

Jim laughed. "Don't build me up too high here. Mom was still there, even if she had to work a lot of long hours. And goodness knows I made a lot of mistakes."

"Everybody does, right? But you didn't quit on those kids. You stuck with them until they were ready to make it on their own." To her surprise, she felt tears prick her eyes. Maybe a few for Jim and the life he'd led, but also a few for herself. For her own upended life and the hard new changes she was learning to make.

Would Katie end up nearly as well as Jim's brother and sisters had? She hoped so. She hoped she would give Katie the love and support Marianne and Toby would have if they'd lived.

Jim reached across the table and took her hand, twining his fingers with hers. She knew she should pull her hand away, but she just couldn't bring herself to do it. "Let's rent a car and drive down to Cove Island Park." His voice was pure, raw seduction.

Now. Now was the time to pull away and say no. It was a crazy idea, for one thing. Despite the bright afternoon sunlight, the day was frigidly cold. And the last thing she needed was more alone time with Jim Mercer. She just had to open her mouth and say no. Period. End of story.

But what came out when she opened her mouth was "Let's do it."

Jim's smile in response came complete with dimples and a wicked glint in his eyes that made her stomach clench with nervous anticipation. "You won't regret it."

But she knew she probably would.

THE DAY WAS much colder than the warm day in late May when Jim and his sister Jen had shared a picnic lunch and walked along the shoreline catching up on all the things they'd missed in each other's lives. But Jim and Lacey had brought warm coats and sturdy walking shoes, so they fared well enough in the waning warmth of the afternoon sun.

Halfway through their walk along the beach, Jim reached for Lacey's hand, expecting her to pull away from his touch. But she merely curled her fingers around his and edged a little closer, until he could feel her warmth cutting through the brisk wind blowing over the water.

She finally gave his hand a tug and came to a stop, turning to look up at him. He was tall enough to block the sunlight making her squint, but enough of the light bathed her face to give her the golden glow of a sea goddess rising from the depths.

That, he thought, was an embarrassingly romantic notion. But he couldn't quite regret it, or the way her hand in his made him feel happy and at peace, despite the turmoil of life around them.

"We need to head back if we're going to get any brainstorming done." Was that a hint of disappointment he heard in her voice?

"I know."

"I'm glad we came here, though." She lifted her face to the breeze, let it blow her hair behind her in glittering golden strands. "It feels sort of magical, you know?"

"I know." He couldn't stop himself from lifting one hand to her cheek, pressing his palm to her cool flesh, letting her hair twist around his fingertips.

"Like anything could happen." She had moved closer, her body scant inches from his. Her gaze wandered away from his to settle on his mouth. "Anything at all."

He lowered his mouth slowly, giving her a chance to pull back. But, instead of moving away, she closed the dwindling distance between them, her lips pressing soft and warm against his mouth.

Magical, he thought, silently echoing her words as he deepened the kiss, tasting the sweet tea and wasabi spice on her tongue. She wrapped her arms around his neck, pressing closer, as if seeking to become part of him the way he wanted to meld himself to her.

It was perfect. It was right. He felt as if all the missing pieces of himself had suddenly fallen into place and he was whole again, the way he hadn't been whole since his father's death. Was such a thing possible? Or was he letting his desire for her, his need to be closer to her, fool him into believing there was more to their connection than really existed.

They'd known each other for days, not months. Surely this sort of feeling took time to build, to grow, to strengthen into something lasting.

And yet, when she curled her fingers through his hair and held him in place while she answered him, kiss for kiss, he felt that nothing in the world could be more right, more lasting, more perfect for him than being with Lacey Miles every day for the rest of his life.

He pulled away first, overwhelmed by the emotions galloping through him, emotions he didn't trust and couldn't reconcile to the reality of his life. Or hers.

She gazed up at him, her expression slightly dazed and wholly recognizable, as if the emotions still beating at his heart like hammer blows were echoing inside her, as well.

"I think we should catch a train home tonight," she whispered.

He nodded. "You're right."

They walked back to the visitor parking lot slowly, not touching, maintaining enough distance that Jim couldn't even feel the heat of her body between him and the sea breeze. But he felt her regardless, felt the steady beat of her presence like a pulse inside his chest. She was inside him, somehow, a part of him that he might never be able to excise.

He didn't know whether that thought thrilled him or terrified him.

Chapter Fifteen

It was after midnight by the time Jim drove the Jeep into the gravel parking area at the side yard of the farmhouse. The house was dark except for the light shining in the front parlor, golden and welcoming.

Cade and Julie Beckett were still awake, fore-warned by a call from Lacey before she and Jim got on the train back to DC. "How'd the trip go?" Cade asked cautiously, as if well aware that their early return might be the result of either good news or bad.

"A mixed bag," Lacey answered, stifling a yawn. "We've eliminated the Whittiers as the car bombers, at least."

"But?" Julie probed.

"But they also provided explanations for a couple of the incidents I've experienced in the past few weeks."

"Which means there's still a threat to Lacey

and Katie," Jim growled, "and we're no closer to knowing who's behind that threat than we were before we went to Connecticut."

Lacey barely resisted the impulse to reach out and take his clenched fist in her hand, to gently ease his tension with her touch. Things between them had escalated rapidly at Cove Island Park, not just physically but emotionally. And it was the emotional connection growing between them that scared her to death.

"Well, I have a new lead for you to follow. Maybe." Julie pulled out her phone and ran her finger across the screen as if searching for something. "While y'all were gone, I contacted a friend of mine, Lanny Copeland, who's a special agent with the Richmond field office. I had this vague memory of a BOLO he'd sent out a few months back about a group of young men from Kaziristan who'd disappeared suddenly right before their student visas expired."

"Sleeper cell?" Jim asked, his muscles twitching as if Julie's words had put him on high alert. Lacey felt her earlier sleepiness drop away as curiosity and a touch of alarm took its place.

"Well, they haven't been considered terrorism suspects, exactly. They all seemed like normal students, westernized and showing no signs of trouble or radicalization. It was really just the fact that they all dropped from the radar right before they were scheduled to return to Kaziristan that pinged Lanny's radar. Okay, here we go." She handed her phone carefully to Lacey. "Does anything in that photo look familiar to you?"

The photo on Julie's phone was a shot of the front of a low-rent apartment complex. The angle was close up on two adjacent apartment doors, numbered 314 and 315, and the paved parking lot in front of the apartments. In the parking slot in front of the apartments were two vehicles, a black panel van that looked to be twenty years old and a later-model blue truck.

A ripple of recognition skated up Lacey's spine. "That's the truck."

"Ever since y'all told me about that truck, it's been nagging at my brain. It seemed so familiar, but I couldn't quite place it, until suddenly I remembered that BOLO for those students and their vehicles. Fortunately, I'd saved the photo to my phone. So I took a look. Sure enough, it fits what you described. Blue Toyota Tacoma, later model, with a dent in the left front panel."

Jim edged closer, looking at the photo over Lacey's shoulder. He felt warm and solid beside her, his nearness easing some of the nervous tension roiling inside her. "Should I call Quinn?" he asked Lacey.

"Already done," Cade said bluntly. He glanced at Lacey. "Sorry if that was presumptuous."

"No, I think the more hands on deck, the better." Kaziri nationals gone missing just before their visas expired could very well mean al Adar was placing sleeper cells in the United States, just as law enforcement had begun to fear.

"He's calling in support from the DC area, but it will probably be morning before anyone can get here." Cade shot them an apologetic look.

"There's one more thing," Julie said, directing her words to Lacey. Her expression held sympathy, but the emotion Lacey saw in the other woman's eyes was darker, angrier. "I called Lanny to tell him about the truck. I explained why I'd thought about it, and he told me something that the FBI hadn't been sharing with other agencies yet. It seems that when the students went missing, something else went missing, as well."

"What's that?"

"Two dozen boxes of screws and ball bearings from the hardware store where one of them worked."

Lacey's knees wobbled. "Oh."

Jim put his arm around her and pulled up one of the chairs across from the sofa. Lacey sat, clenching her hands together as a cold chill ran through her.

"Around the same time, there was an incident at a construction site in southern Maryland. A fire started in a storage area for explosives used to clear large boulders out of road-construction sites. There was a storm that night, and nobody could be sure that one of the lightning strikes in the area hadn't hit the storage site, but of course the FBI had to investigate. The security guard in charge of patrolling the site sustained a concussion, possibly from flying debris from the blast. He doesn't remember anything, including a lightning strike or anything else."

"So it was ruled an accident?"

"Actually, it was ruled inconclusive evidence of a man-made event, but the FBI hasn't ruled out the possibility of human involvement. You see, when the explosives storage hut went up in flames, the resulting blast wasn't quite as large as experts might have expected, leading them to wonder if there might have been substantially less explosive material in the hut than reported."

"Meaning it might have been stolen before the fire destroyed the evidence," Jim said. "Do you know what explosives were stored there?"

"Semtex," Julie answered. She looked at Lacey. "Is that what was used in the explosion that killed your sister?"

"I don't know. The police haven't released that information to the public."

"There aren't that many explosives that would be used in a car bomb, and Semtex is relatively easy to obtain. It just makes sense."

"The car bomb was also packed with ball bearings and sheet-metal screws," Lacey added.

"Which could also be found at a construction site," Jim said.

"That's a hell of a lot of coincidences," Cade muttered.

"Listen, we're not going to solve the mystery of the missing Kaziri students or the purloined explosives tonight," Jim said, his hand warm and firm on Lacey's shoulder. "Let's try to get some sleep and pick this up again in the morning, okay?"

"We think Julie should take Samantha and Katie back to Kentucky with her in the morning." Cade looked at Lacey. "The girls don't need to be here if there's trouble on the way."

"Maybe Lacey should go with them," Jim suggested.

"No way," Lacey said with a shake of her head. "I'm their target, not Katie and not Julie or Samantha. They'd go after us on the way to Kentucky."

"As much as I hate to duck out just when the action starts, I think Lacey's right. It's safest for the girls if she stays here with y'all. By morning, hopefully Quinn will have people here to shore up the security."

"Let's all get to bed, then," Jim said, giving Lacey's shoulder a squeeze. "Tomorrow will be a long day, no doubt."

While Cade and Julie headed down the hall to the guest bedroom, Lacey joined Jim as he went from window to window, door to door, to make sure the place was locked down tightly for the night. When Jim turned out the light in the parlor, plunging the house into darkness, the world outside the window seemed unnaturally bright as the blanket of snow shed an artificial glow across the darkened landscape.

"One good thing," she murmured. "It won't be easy to sneak up on us in all that snow."

"Famous last words." Jim's statement was a grim rumble in the darkness.

THE PHONE RANG just as Jim was starting to release all the tension of the long day and settle into a light doze. The trill shocked him awake, and it took a second to realize what he'd heard.

The number on the display was unfamiliar, and Jim almost hit the ignore button, but the fact that it was a local number gave him pause. He swept his finger across the phone and answered. "Jim Mercer."

"I know it's late," the woman's voice on the other end of the call said without preamble. "I wouldn't have called you except you told me to let you know if anything strange happened."

He tried to place the voice, which sounded familiar. "Who is this?"

"Oh, I'm sorry. It's Charlotte. From the diner in town? I'm the one who told you about that fellow poking around and you gave me your card with your phone number."

"Right." He sat up in his bed, rubbing his fingers through his hair as he tried to wake up. "Has something happened?"

"I'm not sure." She sounded nervous now, as if she'd made the call on impulse and was now second-guessing the decision. "It's probably nothing. You know how small towns can be—everything strange must be a conspiracy. I shouldn't have bothered you so late."

"Charlotte," he said patiently, "tell me why you called."

"Well, now that I think of it, it's silly. And I wouldn't have even seen it if I hadn't gotten up to check and make sure I turned off the oven downstairs in the shop."

"What did you see?"

"It was just odd, you see. We're a little town, and we don't get a lot of traffic coming through the area at this time of night. But while I was down in the shop, I saw four trucks drive by, one after the other, almost like a convoy, you know? It was odd enough that I went outside and watched them go, and one by one, they all took the turn down the road toward the farm. You sure don't get much through traffic, so I thought—"

Her voice cut off suddenly. Jim looked down at his phone and saw that there was no cell signal.

What the hell?

He pulled a pair of jeans out of his dresser drawer and pulled them on, sleep fleeing, replaced by instant alarm. Four trucks heading toward the farm and now he'd lost cell service. Maybe a coincidence.

Maybe not.

He turned on his bedroom light, half expecting that it wouldn't come on. But light blazed brightly in the darkness, making him squint, and he allowed himself a brief moment of relief.

Pushing open the bedroom door, he listened to the familiar noises of the night. The hum of electricity from the refrigerator and the soft whisper of heated air blowing through the vents. The faint ticks and groans of an old house settling in for the night.

He didn't want to wake Lacey, but he needed to know if her cell phone was picking up a signal. To his relief, he saw a light glowing under the door. Tapping lightly on the door, he spoke in a half whisper. "Lacey? It's Jim."

There was a long moment of silence before she answered in just as hushed a tone, "Come in."

She was in bed but awake, dressed in a long-sleeved T-shirt. She was frowning at the phone in her hand. "All my bars disappeared."

He crossed to look at her phone. "Mine, too."

"That's weird, isn't it?" She looked up at him, her brow furrowed. "I thought I heard your phone ring earlier."

"It did." He told her about the call from Charlotte, who ran the diner in Cherry Grove. "It cut off in the middle of her call."

"It wouldn't take long for someone to drive out here from town, would it?" Lacey's gaze slanted toward the window across from her bed, which looked out on the side yard and the parking area.

Jim crossed to the window, staying just wide of the glass. He lifted one edge of the curtain and looked out. With the light on, it was hard to see anything outside even with the glow of the snow-covered land.

"Maybe you should…" Suddenly the light went out in the room. "Turn off the light," he continued.

"I didn't turn off the light," Lacey said, her

voice closer than he expected. He turned his head toward her voice and found her standing beside him, her back pressed against the bedroom wall.

He edged the curtain away from the window again and peered outside. In the side parking area, his Jeep along with the Becketts' Ford Explorer were the only vehicles in sight.

But there was a lot of land surrounding the farm, some of it thick with trees and underbrush. It wouldn't be hard to hide four trucks from view of the road.

"Maybe the lightbulb blew." Lacey's voice was shaky.

Jim crossed to the door and looked out into the hallway. His room was dark as well, even though he'd left his light on.

"My clock is dead. The power is out." Lacey crept closer to him in the dark, her blond hair catching glints of light from the snow glow outside. "I don't suppose the weight of the snow finally snapped a branch and it hit a power line?"

"Nice thought," he answered grimly.

"We'd better tell Cade and Julie."

"Already on it." Cade's voice came from the hallway. He was using a flashlight application on his phone to shed light into the gloom. Julie was right behind him. Already dressed in jeans and a sweater, she had a Ruger tucked into a holster at her side and looked ready for action.

Jim kicked himself for leaving his own room without his Glock. "I'll be right back."

He returned with his Glock holstered at the back of his jeans. "You said you know how to shoot, right?" he asked Lacey.

"Yes, but I don't have a weapon."

"Cade brought an extra," he said with confidence, looking at his former employer with a grin. "Didn't you?"

"Of course." Cade left Lacey's bedroom, plunging it back into darkness.

Jim opened the flashlight app on his own phone and turned it on. It illuminated the tense, worried expression on Lacey's face, and he couldn't stop himself from reaching out to touch her. "We're going to figure out what's going on and we're going to stop it."

"There are four of us and two children," Lacey said with quiet despair. "Maybe we're all armed, but what if they're out there right now, rigging this place to blow? What good will it do for us to go out with guns blazing?"

The truth was, if their communications were jammed and the power had been cut, it was already too late to get out of the house.

Lacey must have read Jim's expression in the

light of the cell-phone app, for she released a soft groan of despair.

Cade returned with a second weapon. "Smith & Wesson SD40. Ten in the mag, one in the chamber. Can you handle it?"

She took the pistol, her expression ambivalent. On the train ride to Stamford earlier that day, she had confessed to Jim that while she had been pretty good with a gun, she'd never really enjoyed shooting. But if it came to having to fire a weapon in order to protect Katie, she'd do it without hesitation.

"I can handle it," she said, and Jim believed her.

"Julie and I will take the north and east windows. You take the south and west." Cade nodded toward the hallway. "Call out if you see anything."

"Should we go to the second floor?" Lacey asked as they headed toward the back of the house. "We might have a better line of sight."

"Good idea." Jim followed her to the narrow staircase at the back of the house that had once been the servants' stairway. Less ornate and grand than the staircase off the parlor, it felt rickety and old beneath his feet. But it held them all the way to the second floor.

"There's a good line of sight from my workroom toward the west," Lacey said as they entered the second-floor hallway. "I'll check there. This back bedroom here looks to the south."

Jim didn't like parting company with her, but they each had a job to do. He peeled off and entered the empty back bedroom, crossing to the curtainless window that looked out on the snowy backyard and the pastureland beyond.

Snow blanketed the area with white, and, while inside the backyard the snow was neither smooth nor pristine thanks to the snowman building earlier in the day, the field beyond was a featureless white void. If anyone had approached the house from that direction, he would see their footprints in the snow.

But that didn't mean there wasn't someone out there. From his vantage point at the window, he couldn't see past the eaves that covered the back porch.

He headed back into the hall to see if he could find a room that wasn't blocked by the eaves. But before he had taken more than a couple of steps, a call rang out from downstairs. It was Cade's voice, sharp with urgency. "Bogeys from the east. At least five."

"Bogeys to the north, as well," Julie called. "I count three on this side."

"Four from the west!" Lacey came out into the hall, her eyes wide with alarm. "I saw four men in white outside, barely visible against the snow."

"My view of the yard closest to the house was blocked by the porch eaves," Jim said, already pushing her toward the front stairs. "But I think we have to assume they're out there, as well."

Lacey stumbled as her foot hit the first stair, and Jim had to grab her to keep her from tumbling down the steps. She clung to him, her grip tight on his arms. In the low light, her gray eyes glittered with fear.

"We're trapped in here, aren't we?" she asked.

He nodded, unable to do anything but tell her the truth. "We are."

Chapter Sixteen

Lacey had been under fire in Afghanistan. She'd waded into the middle of a Baltimore riot to interview protestors. She'd even been caught in a hostage crisis in one of the most dangerous prisons in the world. She'd thought herself nearly bulletproof, and certainly strong enough emotionally and physically to hold her own.

But when she thought about Katie sleeping in her crib downstairs, innocent and unable to protect herself, Lacey knew a fear as profound as any she'd ever known.

When she reached the first floor and came face-to-face with Julie Beckett, she saw a reflection of her own fear in the other woman's eyes. "If they're setting explosives," Julie said urgently, "where is the safest place in this house?"

"Is there such a place if they're setting explosives?" Jim asked, his grip on Lacey's shoulder tightening.

"We have children in here that we have to get out!" Julie turned to her husband. "Cade, we have to get the kids out of here. Can we create a diversion to open up an avenue of escape?"

"No," Cade said, his gaze fixed on a point beyond where they stood. Lacey and the others followed his gaze and saw the flames licking at the wood porch outside the farmhouse. The smell of gasoline hit Lacey's nose around the same time.

"They're burning us out," Jim growled.

Already the air in the house was growing thick with smoke and fumes. Lacey didn't wait another second; she raced down the hallway to Katie's nursery and flung open the door.

Flames climbing the outer walls of the farmhouse cast a flickering glow across the dark room. Lacey reached into the crib and lifted her sleeping niece into her arms, trying to think past her terror to find some sort of solution to their dire problem.

Heat rises to the top. So upstairs was no answer. But maybe the basement would give them some measure of protection? The basement had been the original foundation of the antebellum house that had once stood where the farmhouse now sat, a stone-and-mortar home that would have been built to withstand fires.

But would the musty basement be protection

enough if the house above them burned? Or would it prove another trap from which they couldn't escape?

Jim found her in the doorway of Katie's room. "Julie is getting Samantha. Cade's wetting towels for us to breathe through. There's a stone foundation on this house, isn't there?"

"Yes, but—"

"No buts. There's fire surrounding the house. No breaks in the flames. We looked." He touched Katie's face, then Lacey's. "This is our best hope. Let's do this."

Tugging Katie's sleepy body closer to her, she nodded and followed Jim down the hall to the basement stairs.

"SOMETHING JUST AIN'T RIGHT." Charlotte Brady hadn't been able to get back to sleep after her call to Jim Mercer. The call had cut off in the middle of her words, and when she'd tried to call him back, it had gone straight to voice mail.

"He probably didn't appreciate your calling him in the middle of the blasted night," her husband, George, grumbled into his pillow. "Sort of like I don't appreciate you keeping me awake blathering about it."

"There was something not right about those trucks, and all of a sudden, while I'm trying to tell that man about possible trouble coming his way, the call cuts off? Nope." She pushed herself into a sitting position in the bed and reached for the phone. "I'm calling Roy."

"He ain't gonna be any happier about being jerked out of bed in the middle of the night, either."

"Maybe not. But he knows I'm not one to make up stories." One benefit of having a brother who happened to be the county sheriff.

As George predicted, Roy hadn't been happy about being awakened at two in the morning. But he listened to what Charlotte had to say with interest. He might just be a small-town lawman, but he knew the troubles Lacey Miles had been through in the past few weeks.

He also knew his force might not be enough firepower to handle whatever might be happening out there at the farm. "I'll call in the state boys. We'll get people out there right away to see what's happening."

As she hung up the phone with her brother, Charlotte was beginning to have a sinking feeling that she'd left the call to her brother a little too late.

"WE'VE GOT A couple of 911 calls about a fire out at the old Peabody farm." Roy Dobbins hadn't gotten more than half his order out when the dispatcher interrupted him. "Neighbors in the area called it in, but it sounds like the house is fully involved already. I've sent two trucks out that way."

"Send every deputy available out there, too," Roy ordered, pulling on his uniform pants. Behind him, his wife was already rolling off the bed to head into the kitchen to put on a pot of coffee. "And call in the state police and surrounding counties. This may not just be an ordinary fire."

By the time he'd dressed, Addie had the coffee made. She poured a couple of steaming cups into a thermos and handed it to him on his way to the door. "Come home safe, you hear?"

He kissed her cheek and headed out into the bitter cold, tucking the collar of his uniform jacket more snugly around his neck. He got on the car radio as he turned the heater on high blast and located a deputy already approaching the scene of the fire. "The whole place is up in flames already," Deputy Breyer said loudly, having to compete with the roar of flames and the moan of sirens audible over the radio. "Lots of footprints in the snow around the house, but we couldn't get real close yet. The fire crew has just arrived."

"What about the occupants of the house?"

"No sign of anyone."

Roy's chest tightened with dread.

BOTH CHILDREN WERE CRYING, their soft sobs swallowed by the sounds of rushing flames and crumbling timbers coming from the house overhead. Cade had pushed wet towels into the gap between the heavy oak door and the stairs below, but the fire would soon take those pieces of kindling as surely as it was consuming the beams and floorboards upstairs.

The only light in the basement was the glow from Cade Beckett's cell-phone app, barely enough to see a foot or two in front of their faces. But Lacey was close enough to Jim for him to see the bleak despair in her face as she pressed a damp cloth over Katie's weeping face to keep out the smoke growing inexorably thicker in the small basement.

The howl of sirens outside was muted by the thick stone surrounding them, but Jim knew the fire crew would be looking for survivors. Maybe there was still a chance for rescue.

But not if the house fell in on them, and it sounded as if it was gearing up to do that.

"Is there any other way out of here? Some chink in the foundation where we could dig our way out?" he asked Lacey.

She swung her troubled gaze to his face. "What?"

"This is an old house. Maybe there's a part

of this basement that was patched up recently. We might be able to dig a way out."

She stared at him for a moment, almost uncomprehendingly, before her eyes lit up from inside. "The tunnel."

Cade Beckett moved closer. "What tunnel?"

"When the workers were shoring up the foundation, they found an old tunnel. It's over there, behind that door. I don't know if it leads anywhere, but it's still there, because it's considered a historic artifact. The local historians believe the original house was part of the Underground Railroad. I remember Marianne and Toby were excited to be living somewhere that had such an important role in history."

"And you're sure it hasn't been filled in?"

"No, like I said, it's considered a historical artifact. The builders had to make sure it was structurally sound for the house, and that was it. The historical society was planning to take a better look at the tunnel come spring."

"Let's try it," Julie said, already moving toward the door.

Cade caught her arm. "Wait a second."

"For what? For the house to fall down on top of us? Listen!" She waved toward the ceiling, where the roar of the fire was louder than before. "Let's go, for God's sake. Now!"

The door covering the entrance to the tunnel was made of stone, and it took both Cade and Jim working together to make it budge. They could only pull it open a couple of feet, but that was enough for them all to slip through the opening. "Close it behind us," Lacey urged. "It might stop the fire from entering the tunnel if the house collapses into the basement."

They had barely gotten the door pushed back into place when the ground beneath their feet shook and the sound of breaking timbers and rushing flames penetrated the solid wall of rock. But no sign of flames penetrated the closed door, and only the tiniest tendrils of smoke seeped into the tunnel and floated up to the curved stone ceiling.

Beside Jim, Lacey was trembling wildly as she clutched her crying niece to her chest. Jim wrapped his arms around them both, pressing a kiss against Lacey's forehead. "We're safe for now."

"Do you feel that?" Julie asked.

"What?"

"Cold air. Moving air." She nodded toward the dark mouth of the tunnel ahead. "I think there's air coming in from somewhere ahead. And if there is…"

"Then we may have a way out," Jim finished for her.

ALEXANDER QUINN HAD long ago learned to trust his instincts, even when they seemed to make no sense. It had saved him from a terrorist attack in Iraq in 2003, and from sniper fire in Yemen a few years later.

Tonight, despite the assurance from Cade Beckett that assistance could probably wait for morning, Quinn's instincts had told him he needed to get to Cherry Grove, Virginia, as quickly as he could. Which meant gassing up one of Campbell Cove Security's pair of helicopters with all hands on deck.

The chopper was a modified CH-53E Super Stallion, equipped to carry a combat-ready assault team. Quinn had called in his best men and women for this mission, aware that the quarry they were hunting would be armed and dangerous.

Luckily, so were his agents.

His pilot landed the Super Stallion in a flat field about a half mile north of the Cherry Grove farmhouse just a few minutes past two in the morning. To Quinn's dismay, the glow on the snowy horizon suggested they might be too late to help his imperiled agents.

But they had another mission, already approved by an in-air radio call to one of the top commanders in the Virginia State Police, who happened to be an old friend of Quinn's from his days in the CIA. Ethan Tolliver had been an FBI legat before he'd taken the job with the state police, and he and Quinn had shared many a drink and a tall tale at the US embassy in Turkey when they'd both been assigned there in the late nineties.

"I'll let all the locals know you're coming in hot," Tolliver had assured him after catching him up on all that had happened since their liftoff back in Kentucky. "We've got unknown targets out there, probably up to no good. You folks try to hunt them down, and we'll do all we can to get your people out of that house."

Quinn gave the glow on the horizon another grim look, then barked orders at his team. "They'll still be around here somewhere. Track them down. And bring them all in. Alive is better than dead." He checked the magazine of his Ruger. "We have some questions we need answered."

THOUGH IT FELT as if they had been walking forever, a glance at her watch told Lacey that it had been only a half hour or so, each step taking them closer and closer to the source of the icy air that seemed to permeate her bones until her teeth chattered uncontrollably.

Jim had taken Katie from her earlier, wrapping his big frame around the little girl to keep her warm. Before they'd headed into the basement, Jim had been clearheaded enough to grab coats for them all, while Julie did the same for her family, so even though they were all cold enough to shiver in the frigid tunnel, they weren't likely to reach full hypothermia before they reached the end of the tunnel.

But what then? She had no idea where the tunnel came out, if it came out at all. Would they have to dig their way through some sort of collapse at the end? Or would the tunnel open into the snowy woods, where they'd have no protection from the elements at all.

"I think I see it." Cade stretched his cell phone toward the darkened tunnel ahead, and Lacey saw it, too. A steep stairway built of stone, extending upward into a hole in the roof of the tunnel.

"Wait," Lacey said as the others started moving faster toward the stairs. "Just because the people who burned us out of the house probably didn't stick around after it started to collapse, that doesn't mean they're not still out there somewhere, waiting for final confirmation that we died in the fire."

"She's right." Jim shifted Katie in his arms, tugging her even closer to him. "If we're right about those people out there being some sort of al Adar sleeper cell sent to take out Lacey, they won't go away until they have some sort of evidence to show for their actions."

"They'll want confirmation that I'm dead," Lacey said flatly. "They're out there, waiting to see the bodies pulled from the ashes."

"Well, we can't stay down here and freeze to death," Julie protested, hugging Samantha closer. The little girl had stopped crying, but she still looked terrified. Lacey wished they had a way to deal with their reality without terrifying the little girls, but they didn't have the luxury for anything but blunt talk at this point.

"Jim and I can go out there and scout around," Cade suggested. "See if we spot anyone."

"What about your cell phone?" Lacey asked. "Are you getting a signal now?"

Cade peered at the display. "No. But the stone walls may be blocking it. I need to get outside and see if I get any bars."

"If they're hanging around, they may still be jamming cell signals," Julie warned.

"We have to take a chance." Jim turned to look at Lacey, his expression intense. "You and Julie keep the children down here. Cade and I will go out and see what we're up against."

She shook her head. "None of you would be out here if it weren't for me. I'm the one they want dead. I can't send you out there like cannon fodder while I hide down here in safety."

"Lacey—"

"Let her go," Julie said flatly. "It's her fight as much as it's any of yours. I'll keep the girls safe down here."

"No." Jim shook his head. "There's no reason for you to martyr yourself, Lacey. Katie needs you alive."

"She needs us both alive. Both of us. I can't just send you out there for me, don't you get that? If something happened to you because I stayed back here like a coward... I'm going. We're going to find a way to safety. And then we're coming back for the others. End of story." Lacey leaned forward and gave Katie's cold cheek a swift, fierce kiss, her heart feeling so full she feared it would explode.

Jim closed his eyes for a long moment, his expression pained. Then he kissed the top of Katie's blond curls and handed the little girl to Julie. "Take care of my Katiebug."

"Y'all be careful," Julie said, lifting her face for her husband's kiss. "I'll keep these rug rats safe and warm, I promise."

Jim went up the stairs first, pausing as his head breached the top. He swiveled his face slowly, twisting on the stairs until he could see all the way around. He dipped his head back below the hole. "I don't see any movement, but we can't assume there's not someone out there."

"Just be careful when you go out, okay?" Lacey stood at the bottom of the stairs, waiting for her turn to go. Once she saw Jim's feet disappear through the hole, she started up behind him.

The stone steps were slick with moisture and age, making it hard to keep her footing. She had pulled on sneakers rather than boots when Jim woke her, not expecting to have to trek through the snowy woods. But it was better than being barefoot, she supposed.

Like Jim, she paused at the top of the exit and took a look around. The tunnel came out in thick woods that would have been thicker still with summer foliage. As it was, there were enough evergreen trees and bushes to make the woods around them seem nearly impenetrable. Snow here lay only in scabrous patches, the forest floor protected by the trees overhead from the worst of the snowfall.

On the downside, there were plenty of places for wrongdoers to lie in wait.

Jim caught her hand and helped her up the rest of the way, practically lifting her off her feet to set her on the ground beside him. He put his arm around her, lending her his warmth. His eyes never stopped moving, scanning the woods around them as they waited for Cade Beckett to finish climbing the stone stairs.

"Where do you think we are?" Cade asked when he pulled himself out of the tunnel mouth.

"I'm not sure," Lacey confessed. "I think we're still on farm property, since the historical society didn't tell Marianne and Toby that they shared the tunnel with anyone else. If so, we're probably in the woods on the southern edge of the property. The town is about a mile east of here. If you can figure out what direction east would be."

"Any cell signal?" Jim asked Cade.

"No," he answered with a frown. "Those signal jammers don't have that large a range…"

"Which means they're still close," Lacey said, hair rising on the back of her neck.

"Very close," Jim said in a strangled tone, his gaze fixed somewhere behind her.

Lacey turned and saw three figures dressed in arctic camouflage moving toward them at a wary pace. Each was armed with a hunting rifle, though none of them, Lacey noticed, seemed at ease with the weapons.

Burning people in their beds more your style, cowards?

Jim and Cade had their weapons up before Lacey could blink, but at best, it was a standoff. And since rifles were far more accurate at a distance, they weren't looking at a best-case scenario.

She pulled the borrowed SD40 from the holster at her side and aimed it at the slowly approaching figures.

Suddenly, the woods lit up as bright as daylight. The approaching men froze in confusion as the woods erupted with a dozen men, similarly clad in arctic camo, emerging from their hiding places with weapons raised.

"What the hell?" Lacey asked, staring as the newcomers surrounded the other three men, shouting orders in Kaziri to lay down their weapons.

"That," Cade Beckett said with a spreading smile, "is why it pays to have Alexander Quinn for a boss."

Chapter Seventeen

"That's the problem with recruiting westernized kids," Alexander Quinn said with a grim smile, turning away from the monitor showing the occupants of interview room four at the Virginia State Police barracks a county over from Cherry Grove. "They never can keep their traps shut."

"So, Ghal Rehani is the one who put a hit on Lacey?" Jim asked. "Because she insulted him on air by calling him a self-proclaimed warlord?"

"I think it was the 'self-proclaimed' part that pissed him off," Quinn said. "I just got a call from an old friend in the Federal Police. They picked up Rehani about an hour ago."

Jim was still shaking his head. "I don't want to be the one to tell Lacey her sister and brother-in-law were killed because some Osama bin Laden wannabe got his little feelings hurt."

"It would be nice, wouldn't it, if it took a

lot more than a schoolyard put-down to push a man to murderous rage?" Quinn put his hand on Jim's shoulder. "You did a good job, Mercer. I think you're going to be a real asset at Campbell Cove Academy." He paused as he reached the door of the office. "That is, if you want to keep working with us."

"I have a lot of decisions to make," Jim said. It wasn't exactly an answer to Quinn's implied question, but it was as much as he could offer until he had a chance to talk to Lacey and find out what her plans were for her and Katie.

He found her in the barracks commander's office, curled up asleep on one end of a small sofa, with Katie napping in her arms. Grimy and rumpled, with soot staining her hair and dark circles of exhaustion under her eyes, she was a mess. But he'd never seen anything more beautiful than the steady rise and fall of her breathing, a potent reminder of what he almost lost tonight.

At his desk, the barracks commander, who'd introduced himself as Ethan Tolliver when the county sheriff had delivered Jim, Lacey, Katie and the Becketts to the state police division headquarters, looked up from the paperwork spread across his desk. He put one finger to his lips and waved Jim over to the chair in front of his desk.

"Long night," Tolliver said quietly.

"You have no idea."

"Where are you folks going to go now? You have a place to stay?"

Jim rubbed his gritty eyes. "My boss has reserved some rooms for us in a local hotel. We're good for now."

"Reckon you all lost about everything in the fire."

Jim looked at Lacey and Katie curled around each other in slumber. "Not everything."

Tolliver followed Jim's gaze. "No, not everything."

"Any idea when you're cutting us loose from here? I could use a shower and about a week of sleep."

"I'm signing the papers now. I'll deliver them up to the front desk myself, and then you'll be free to go, though I'd appreciate it if you stick around the area for a few more days until we finish up the investigation."

Jim's gaze trailed back to Lacey. "I'm not going anywhere."

A knock on the door made Lacey stir. She sat up, her sleepy gaze locking with Jim's. "Hey."

"Hey," he said with a smile.

At Tolliver's bidding, a young uniformed state police officer entered the room, sparing a quick glance at Jim and Lacey before he looked back at the division commander. "There's an FBI agent here to see you."

Tolliver sighed. "I'm from the government, and I'm here to help," he muttered as he headed out the door.

Jim didn't bother reminding him he was also part of the government. He supposed every layer of bureaucracy probably resented the layers above.

Lacey nuzzled Katie's curls and stifled a yawn. "What's happening?"

"The state police are about to spring us."

"Yay." She made a face. "Where do we go now?"

"Quinn got us some hotel rooms. I guess we go shower and try to catch up on a little sleep."

"What about the guys they captured?"

"Quinn thinks they got them all, based on the numbers we saw outside. We can't be sure how many were on the southern side of the house, since the eaves blocked my view, but we figure at most there were four on that side, and we saw twelve others. They picked up sixteen men, so that fits."

"Have any of them said anything yet?"

"One of them told everything he knows. His story's being checked out, of course, but it rings true."

Her brow furrowed. "Why did they target

me? Was it the story I did on Tahir Mahmood, speculating that he wasn't dead?"

Jim shook his head. "It was a report you did a couple of months ago on the rise of strongmen in the Kaziri countryside, the ones who were aligning themselves with al Adar in hopes of improving their standing in their villages."

Her frown deepened. "Why on earth would someone target me for that?"

Damn, he didn't want to tell her what he'd learned. But better from him than from someone who didn't care about her and how much she'd lost. "You called Ghal Rehani a self-proclaimed warlord."

She stared at him for a moment, looking puzzled. Then, suddenly, the realization dawned, and her mouth dropped open. "Oh, my God. You cannot be serious."

"I know it sounds crazy..."

"It is crazy. He's crazy. He put a hit on me for that? Because, what? I hurt his little feelings?" She got up suddenly, jostling Katie, who began to cry. Shoving Katie into Jim's arms, Lacey hurried out of the office, slamming the door behind her.

Jim wanted to follow, but he knew she needed time to process the truth about her sister's death. A small man's outsize vanity had cost Lacey her sister and brother-in-law. It had stolen

Katie's parents from her life. It had left the world a smaller, meaner place, and nothing Jim could say or do would change that reality.

He pressed soft kisses against Katie's cheek, murmuring words of comfort. Eventually, she curled her hands in the collar of his jacket and snuggled close as he rocked her from side to side.

LACEY STOOD OUTSIDE in the frigid predawn, gazing up at the stars overhead and wanting to scream at the universe. Her voice seemed trapped in her throat, tears beating frantically at the backs of her eyes but unable to escape and give her any sort of release.

The world was insane. The people inhabiting it were petty and cruel, venal and ridiculous. Deaths were meaningless and lives cut short for no good reason at all.

It wasn't fair. It wasn't right.

It was all her fault.

She heard the door behind her open and footsteps move toward her. She steeled herself for Jim's voice, but it was Julie Beckett who came to stand beside her. She lifted her face to the sky as well, gazing up at the stars.

"This world sucks," Julie said.

"Yeah, it does."

"Except when it doesn't." Julie looked away

from the stars, focusing her gaze on Lacey. "It's so easy to get drawn into the evil and insanity we come across every day in this business. You as a reporter. Me as a cop, of sorts."

"I used to think I was making a difference, you know?" Lacey pushed her hair back from her face, feeling as if all the grief in the world was bottled up inside her. "I thought what I did mattered."

"It does. You tell the truth, however harsh and unwanted it may be. That matters a lot."

She shook her head. "A careless choice of words got my sister and brother-in-law killed."

"No." Julie caught Lacey's arm and pulled her around until they were face-to-face. Julie's eyes blazed with anger. "A stupid, evil man sent other stupid, evil men to kill you. That's what happened. I'm terribly sorry about your sister and brother-in-law. I am. But if you give in to that man's evil, if you accept the blame instead of putting it square where it belongs, who wins? Not you. Not Katie. Not Marianne or Toby. Ghal Rehani wins, because you've validated his world view. Don't do that, Lacey. Do not do that."

"She's right." Jim's voice rumbled from the darkness. He came out of the shadows near the door, his arms wrapped around Katie. "You can't give up. Not on any of it."

Lacey closed her burning eyes. "Are we free to go yet?"

"Yeah. Quinn's already given me the keys to our hotel room." He looked at Julie. "Somehow, our vehicles survived without damage. He's had them delivered to the visitor parking area here. Cade has the keys. He and Samantha will meet you there."

"Wait," Lacey said as Julie started toward visitor parking. "Can you guys take Katie with you? There's somewhere I want to go first, before I head for the hotel."

Jim frowned. "You're ready to drop, Lacey. You need a shower and sleep. Whatever it is you want to do, can't it wait?"

She shook her head. "I need you to take me somewhere. Please."

Whatever he saw in her face seemed to melt his opposition. He handed Katie to Julie. "Katie-bug, Julie's going to take you to play with Samantha for a little while. Wouldn't you like that?"

Katie looked up at him with bleary eyes, but she gave only a token protest when Julie pulled her from Jim's arms. She quickly settled into a snuggle against Julie's shoulder.

Julie smiled at them. "I love them when they're this age. Makes me want to have another one."

Lacey watched until Julie disappeared around

the corner of the building. Then she turned to look at Jim. "Thank you for doing this. I know you must be exhausted."

"We all are. But I'm never going to be able to sleep until I know you're safe at the hotel."

She touched his arm, her fingers trailing down across his before she dropped her hand to her side. "It might be easier if I drive."

He handed over the keys to the Jeep and followed her to the visitor parking lot. "Are you sure you're awake enough to drive?"

"Believe me, I won't be able to sleep at all until I do this."

THE CEMETERY WAS small and secluded, tucked away behind an old stone church about five miles from where the farmhouse had stood in Cherry Grove. Lacey parked the Jeep haphazardly just outside the ornate iron gate that guarded the graveyard's entrance.

Jim wasn't sure he should follow, but Lacey motioned for him to join her. She caught his hand as they stepped into the graveyard and picked their way among the engraved headstones.

The stone straight ahead was new, gleaming brightly among the other weathered stones. Lacey's grip on Jim's hand tightened, and he locked his fingers with hers, offering her all the strength he had.

"I wanted to come here one day and tell her we found the people who killed her," Lacey murmured, her voice almost as hushed as the cemetery surrounding them. "I didn't think it would end this way. It was all so incredibly senseless."

"Most murders are," Jim said.

She looked up at him. "It's not fair."

"No. It's not."

"All Ken Calvert wanted was to see his kids more, and now he's dead. It's so stupid."

"It is," Jim agreed.

"I think he wanted to see me that night because he found out about Ghal Rehani's vendetta. Central Asia is his beat. He'd have wanted to give me a heads-up, even though it was probably considered classified information." She looked down at her sister's grave. "I wonder if he'd still be alive if he hadn't tried to meet me that night."

The moon had finally broken through the clouds just as it was ready to leave the sky and give way to morning, lending just enough light for Jim to see the tears welling in Lacey's eyes before they spilled in silver tracks down her cheeks.

A hard sob escaped her lips, followed by another. Then another. Jim reached for her, pulling her into the shelter of his arms, letting her spill her grief on his strong shoulders.

When she was spent, she melted into his embrace, her breathing slowly subsiding to normal. The cold began to seep through their clothing, and Jim gave her a gentle nudge. "We're going to freeze to death out here."

She nodded, rubbing her face against his damp shirt. "Can you drive back?"

"Of course."

They didn't talk on the way to the hotel. Lacey seemed completely drained, and Jim didn't know what to say to her that would make her feel any better. He just hoped it was enough to be there with her, ready if she needed him. He hoped when she found her feet again, she'd want him at her side.

He parked the Jeep in the hotel parking lot and cut the engine. "We're here."

She stirred, lifting her head from where it had rested against the window for most of the trip back. "Oh."

When she made no move to get out of the vehicle, he walked around the Jeep and opened the door for her, giving her his hand to help her out. She twined her fingers with his, huddling close as if for warmth while they checked in at the front desk. His room was next to Lacey's, he saw with relief. He didn't think he could bear being far from her tonight.

He wasn't sure he could bear it any night, ever again.

She unlocked her hotel door and pushed it open, revealing a clean, spacious room with two double beds. She shrugged off her jacket and tossed it on one bed, her nose wrinkling. "Definitely need a shower."

"You sure you'll be okay? You want me to find the Becketts and get Katie for you?"

She turned to look at him. "I'll be okay. Let Katie sleep."

Reluctantly, he backed out of the room, letting her close the door and shut him out. He trudged the few feet between their rooms and let himself into his own hotel room.

The hot shower felt like heaven, sluicing away the grime and soot from their ordeal. He could still smell the smoke and knew he probably would for a few days to come, but at least none of them had experienced any smoke-inhalation problems. The paramedics on the scene had checked them all, paying extra attention to the children. Everyone was fine.

Thank God for abolitionists, he thought, still protecting the pursued even now.

Somehow, Alexander Quinn had provided clean clothing that actually fit Jim's lean-muscled build. He pulled on a clean pair of boxer shorts and was contemplating whether to put on a T-shirt as well when there was a knock on the door. He crossed to open it, expecting to find his boss on the other side.

But it was Lacey who stood on the other side of the door.

She'd showered and dressed in a clean pair of shorts and a long-sleeved T-shirt. Her hair hung in damp strings around her shoulders and her face was scrubbed clean.

"I love you," she said.

He stood in stunned silence, certain he'd misunderstood.

"I don't expect you to say it back, or even feel the same way. It's okay if you don't. I just couldn't let any more time go by without saying it. There are so many things I wish I'd said to Marianne and Toby, things I won't get to say to them, not in this life. I didn't want to make the same mistake with you."

She turned as if to go, but he caught her hand, tugging her back around to face him. "I love you, too. And it's okay if you don't know what to do with that, or what to do with how you feel. I don't need any promises or plans right now. I just need you to know I feel the same way."

She closed the distance between them in one swift step, throwing her arms around his waist and burying her face in his chest. He held her close, pressing soft, fervent kisses in her damp hair. "I love you, Lacey. I love Katie, too. And whatever happens next, nothing is gonna change that. You hear me?"

When she lifted her face to his, she was smiling through her tears. "I hear you."

He slowly lowered his mouth to hers, giving her time to back away if she wanted. The timing was all wrong, but he couldn't hold back the way he felt about her, letting his lips and tongue convey the complexity of emotions, of love and desire and commitment all tangled into one heady elixir.

She kissed him back, and in every brush of her lips, every stroke of her tongue against his, he felt his love for her returned with equal intensity.

She finally pulled back, ending the kiss, and gazed up at him with the first hint of joy he'd ever seen in her eyes. "I'm going to sleep with you tonight, Jim Mercer. Just sleep." Her kiss-stung lips quirked. "Sorry about that part."

He took her hand and led her to the nearest bed, smiling up at her as he sat on the edge and took her hands. "I'm not. I'm not sorry at all."

Epilogue

Four months was long enough.

Lacey had been busy during that span of time, negotiating a lighter schedule with the network and trying to make her Arlington condo work for life with a two-year-old. And there was Jim, of course, as constant in her life now as he'd promised. He and Katie had healed a lot of her wounds, the ones that had scarred her life when her sister died and a few she hadn't even realized she had, from a life lived constantly on the edge, looking for something she couldn't define.

She'd found it, finally, in the one place she'd never thought to look—inside herself. In her absolute adoration for her niece and her deepening, broadening love for the man who'd showed her that true love wasn't some unreachable, unknowable fairy tale but something constant and real, in good times and bad. They'd married a couple of weeks ago, had run off to a cheesy little wedding chapel in the Smoky Mountains and tied the knot. Jim's family had been there, as loving and welcoming as Jim himself, and Katie had taken her job as flower girl seriously, carpeting the wedding-chapel aisle with rose petals so thickly that she ran out halfway up the aisle.

She was Mrs. Jim Mercer now. Lacey Miles-Mercer.

She liked it. A lot.

It had been Jim who'd convinced her it was time to go back to Cherry Grove. Whether the house was still there or not, the farm remained, and she needed to make some decisions about it.

"This place looks so different," she commented as they drove through the middle of Cherry Grove.

"And exactly the same," Jim said with a grin as they passed the diner and waved at Charlotte Brady, who was sweeping the sidewalk in front of the store.

Winter had passed and spring was in full flower, the trees thick with their new green foliage and flowers blooming in pots and hedges in front of every building along Main Street.

Lacey found her stomach clenching with nerves as they made the turn down the road to the farm. Here, too, was a world reborn, the grass in the pastureland green and lush. One day, Lacey remembered, Marianne and Toby had planned to buy some horses to graze the pastures. Maybe a milk cow and some goats and chickens to supplement their supply of food.

Everything looked familiar and strange at the same time, but the overwhelming sense that seeped its way into her consciousness was that she was coming home.

She had lived here only a short month, but it had become part of her in a way that caught her completely by surprise.

Wrapped up in pondering what that unexpected feeling meant, it took her longer than it should have to realize that the blackened, ravaged ruin she had been bracing herself to see was no longer there.

In its place stood the half-built frame of a new farmhouse, surrounded by a crew of construction workers hard at work rebuilding the structure that had so recently burned to the ground.

"What…what?" Lacey stared at the rising bones of the new house, then back at Jim. He smiled at her, his hazel-green eyes twinkling with mischievous joy.

"Surprise," he said.

"How… I haven't even cashed the insurance check yet."

"You were going to put that toward Katie's

college fund, so I thought maybe I should find another way to rebuild the house."

"What other way?"

"You knew when I swept you into an elopement last month there were still a few things you hadn't yet learned about me. Well, one of them was that I recently sold a piece of land in North Carolina that I'd bought after my first year in the Marine Corps. Since I wasn't planning on going to college at that point, my mother gave me the savings she and my dad had put away for my schooling, and I bought land to build a house after I got out of the Marine Corps. It was sitting there, undeveloped, for a long time. Until a land developer decided he wanted it for a new subdivision he was planning." Jim grinned. "Paid a bloody fortune for it. More than five times what I paid for it."

"And you, what? Used your money to rebuild the farmhouse?"

"It was your sister's dream. It was supposed to be Katie's home. I know you have other plans now, other dreams, but I thought at least Katie could have a place that connected her to her parents. If you don't want to do anything with it, the farmland could be rented out, and we could just keep the house as a vacation spot or something."

She stared at him, her heart so full she could barely find her voice. "How do you do that?"

He touched her cheek. "Do what?"

"Know what I want before I even know I want it?"

He bent to kiss her, a long, sweet, promising kiss that made her head spin and her heart soar. "Because I love you."

In the car seat behind them, Katie was growing impatient. "Home!" she said in a loud, insistent voice.

Lacey gave Jim a last, sweet kiss and turned to look at the farmhouse rising from the ashes.

"That's right, baby," she said. "We're home."

* * * * *

Get 2 Free Books,
Plus 2 Free Gifts—

just for trying the
Reader Service!

Get 2 Free Books,
<u>Plus</u> 2 Free Gifts—
just for trying the Reader Service!